THE iNViTATION

Con Shalevski

First published by Busybird Publishing 2024

ISBN:
Paperback: 978-1-922954-52-7
Ebook: 978-1-922954-53-4

Cover image: Karen Kirby, Alby Finn Nash (hand model)

Cover design: Busybird Publishing

Layout and typesetting: Busybird Publishing

Busybird Publishing
2/118 Para Road
Montmorency, Victoria
Australia 3094
www.busybird.com.au

'invitation'

a written or verbal request inviting someone to go somewhere or to do something.

'a wedding invitation'

the action of inviting someone to celebrate two people vowing to spend a lifetime together.

'a ghost tour (by invitation only)'

a situation or action that tempts someone to do something or makes a particular outcome likely.

'tactics like those at the Oscar's would have been an invitation to disaster'

The first invitation began in the 12th Century with a town crier, who would walk and announce important events to the public. Word of mouth was an important means of spreading news, and anyone within hearing of the town crier was, by default, invited to that event.

Nowadays, people tend to invite others not only by traditional invitation, but also by email, text, phone, or the old-fashioned way, word of mouth.

For my dad, and brother, Sam.

I miss you both dearly.

Contents

THE

GHOST

TOUR

Chapter 1

I always kick off the morning with a coffee. I have done so for the past fifteen years. I love that wonderful feeling once the caffeine hits my insides. I can count the number of times I've missed my morning coffee on one hand.

One time, back when I owned a car, it had broken down on the freeway while I was heading to work. I was stuck out there in the emergency lane for over three hours. The RACV and tow truck took their bloody time getting out to me. By the time they had arrived, I had passed the point of frustration and entered into the world of anger – angry because my bloodstream had no coffee running through it. The towie got the full brunt of my temper and disturbing vocabulary.

The second time I had suffered without a coffee was when my ex-wife's waters broke and I had to rush her to the hospital. I stayed with her the entire time she was in labour. She didn't want me to leave her side. My moods and temper when around her seemed to escalate to another level. Without coffee, dangerous.

The birth of my girl was the single most exciting time in my life. The second was my divorce. Sad but true.

And the third time was yesterday. I'd had a long night – drinks after work ended at 2:00 in the morning. I slept through two alarms and didn't get out of bed until 11:00am. Luckily, work was understanding about it. There are many teachers who can stand in for someone at short notice. Not proud of it, but they've sat in for me a few times in the past.

'Latte for Chad.'

My coffee is ready. Chad isn't my real name. I use a different name every time I order coffee. Like a pseudonym. It gives me an opportunity to be whoever I want to be. I've used Chad a few times. I like that name. I've used it when I meet new people, too. Chad makes me more handsome. Girls like that name. 'Hi, my name is Chad.'

There is a ring to it, don't you think?

I'm glad it's Friday, and I'm glad there is no school on weekends. The most exciting part of my day is when I leave to go home.

Some of the kids can be really nasty. All the talking and name calling behind my back. I've been called every name under the sun. Sometimes, I get the urge to fight back. I've had to fight an impulse to punch a couple of them in the face. Jab a few fingers into their throats. Back when I went to school we called that a 'throatie'. I know it sounds terrible, but no one knows the difficulties of being a teacher unless you are one. These little shits can push all your wrong buttons.

I'm a mathematics teacher at Parade College in Bundoora. I catch the tram every morning from my house in Preston. Being two blocks from the closest tram stop on Plenty Road makes things so convenient. I save money on not owning a car; no rego, insurance, petrol, service, maintenance, parking fines – no worries. Uber simplifies the need to go any further than the tram allows me to. If it's not on the tram path, I tend to not go. Number one rule. My rule.

I make my way over to the counter to get my coffee. There is a large lady in a blue uniform in front of me. I think she's a nurse, or something.

She moves from the counter and I move in. I grab my coffee and throw the barista a smile. The cup is nice and warm against my palm and fingers. The smell of the freshly-brewed coffee makes my insides tingle. My nose is in heaven. Paradise with every sip.

The lady in the blue uniform has opened the door to leave the café when I see a sheet of paper fall from her bag and float towards the tiled floor. She leaves before she notices.

I pick it up and read the headline.

Invite only – Ghost Tour.

This could be that exciting thing I've been waiting for. A boredom changer; the most exciting thing in my life since the divorce.

But I decide to hand it back – the invite is not mine, and it wasn't meant for me. I step out of the busy cafe, looking both ways, and I see her turn the corner. I break into a slow jog to catch up. But when I turn the corner, she's not there. As if she vanished into thin air. Where could she have gotten to?

I walk back to the café. I'll just hand it to the people behind the counter and tell them I found it on the floor. But my evil twin in my head is telling me to put it in my bag and take it home – read it, sleep on it, and return it on Monday. Surely that should be, okay … shouldn't it?

I hop on the tram. I have an hour before the first period and the school is about ten minutes away. I've still got heaps of time. I take a seat with my coffee in one hand and the invite in the other. I look out the window, at everyone moving robotically about their day, and all I can think about is the invite in my hand.

Chapter 2

I'm daydreaming about something that I simply can't remember, and I miss my stop. Now I'm heading towards the end of the line. I can't believe no one reminded me; I see the same people almost every day, they know where I get off! Frustrated, I stand and press the button.

Once upon a time people would sit next to you and strike up a conversation. It used to kill travel time and boredom. Nowadays, everyone sits on their devices, their fingers madly typing. They are submerged into social media and all of the other crap on their phones. They've forgotten how to socialise. It's funny to say this, but I miss the good old days when phones weren't even a thought, and the only form of communication was face to face.

I switch to a tram going back towards work. A large number of people get off at my stop, but the doors close on me when I go to exit. I lift my hands up in protest to the driver as a 'WTF dude?' The doors reopen for a pregnant lady, but the driver didn't even notice me getting off, or my arms raised in protest. So fucking annoying.

I cross the road and make my way into the school grounds. I've passed through the carpark and am heading towards the main building before

I realise I'm not holding the invite. I must have dropped it somewhere, or I have left it on the tram.

I sprint back to the tram stop, but the tram is long gone. I think about what to do next. None of my peers have seen me yet, which gives me an idea. I'll email the head coordinator letting him know I won't be in. I can tell them that my doctor has rung me and wants to see me in person to talk about some results. I haven't been feeling the best of late.

I can't tell them the truth – they'll think I'm crazy. How would you react if I told you, 'I'm not coming in today because I left an invitation to a ghost tour that doesn't belong to me on the tram?' I'd be the laughing stock of the staff room. No, I think I'll stick to the doctor story. I'll email them once I've retrieved the invite.

Plenty Road at that time of the morning is busy. Three lanes of heavy metal machinery driving well over the speed limit. It's like playing Frogger – you're the frog and the cars are what you need to watch out for.

I can see a cab approaching from a distance. It's in the middle lane. If I flag it down, I can overtake the tram and meet it at the stop in front. I signal for the cab to stop. He drives past me. Stupid driver. He had no passengers in there. Why didn't he stop? Maybe he didn't see me … he was in the middle lane, probably didn't notice me waving. I'll keep walking to the next stop until another one comes by.

But no other taxis pass. I wait at the stop for the next tram heading towards the city. As I wait, I notice a piece of paper on the tracks. My eyes are a little out of focus and I can't see it clearly. The sheet of paper is face down, the writing not visible. I look both ways to see if a tram is coming. Last thing I need right now is to be hit by a tram trying to retrieve a piece of paper from the tracks.

I'm the only one at the stop. I walk on to the track and retrieve the paper.

It's the invite.

How do you explain this? Fate? It was meant to be.

But how did it make its way onto the tracks? Maybe a gust of wind swept through the cabin and blew it out the doors. Or someone picked it up, read it, and tossed it as they'd exited. Nevertheless, I have it in my hand and it's a sign telling me I should go.

Is there a name on it? Maybe this is a personal invite and only they're permitted to go. I have a quick glance. There's no name on it. Excellent. But I might just head home and read it carefully before I respond to anything, look into it a little further. It could be fake, someone trying to embezzle money from me.

Then it crosses my mind that I haven't paid for it. I haven't paid for anything.

I hop on the next tram that comes by. I'll get home and work it out while I make myself breakfast. Firstly, I need to email the school and let them know I'll be absent today. Mr. Kluger, or Krueger, as the students call him, won't be too impressed with me. The students call him that for a few reasons. The two I know of are his surname sounds like Krueger, and he can be just as nasty and mean as Freddy. But my care factor right this minute is zero.

I get to my apartment block and buzz myself in. I bought this place after my separation. The little money I walked away with helped me secure it. Mi casa.

I put the key in the lock and jiggle it around. Since the break in the lock has been somewhat troublesome. I just haven't gotten around to fix it yet. It's been four years already. How time flies when you aren't having fun.

My mind goes blank from time to time. I feel like someone has slowly erased bits of my memory so I won't remember things. I kind of don't mind that. Could you imagine if you remembered everything, every detail of your past? Bad things have happened in mine, I know they have. I just can't remember them. I really don't have the desire to.

It's why I don't remember much about the break in. Thieves took almost everything but the cutlery, pots and pans, a recliner, and my bed, some bathroom stuff and some of my clothes. I haven't replaced anything. I got used to living like this. It's really fun living with the bare minimum. Actually, this is well under bare minimum.

I watch movies, the news, and scroll social media on my laptop now. I have Facebook. I have eleven followers and I follow over three hundred. I haven't posted anything since the time I was burgled. Maybe they knew where I lived because of my posts; the inside of my apartment spread across every photo.

My number one follower is my daughter, Sia, short for Anastasia. She lives with her mum in Brisbane. I don't get to see her as often as I would like. We haven't spoken for a while. My fault. I want to patch things up but I'm not sure how to go about it. I need to work out what I did wrong first. I should ask her. She'll tell me. Very outspoken, like her mum.

I've reached out and messaged her a couple of times but I haven't had a response, yet. I'm still waiting for the day I do.

I open my laptop and bring it to life. I email Krueger – I mean Kluger. I must be careful I don't write that. Boy, I'd be in deep trouble. And ... sent. Gone. Travelling with super speed through the frequency to his computer. It's amazing how these devices work.

I take my shoes off and put on my slippers. I walk into the kitchen and get myself a glass of water. The coffee taste is still lingering on my buds. That beautiful taste.

I look over my right shoulder towards a photo in a frame on the kitchen bench. It's a photo of Sia. The photo was taken a while back. I imagine her looking the same, only slightly older. I miss her.

I bring myself back to the present and reach into my bag to take out the invitation. I wonder if the lady has noticed it missing from her bag? What if she was looking forward to it? I need to stop thinking about that. This invite is in my possession now.

I glance over it. My eyes wander like a guy's would in The Men's Gallery; so many delicious items on offer. I look once again in case there is a name secretly attached to it, but the only name I see is from the organiser – the person who will conduct the tour. His name is Dr. Samuel Lichtenstein. I wonder what he's a doctor of? Probably Ghost Whispering. I laugh a little. Maybe he can speak to the dead. That would be cool.

You are invited to the experience of your lifetime.

A ghost tour like no other. Deadly serious.

Don't be late.

Invite only. Present this invitation for admission.

Come alone, come prepared, come ready to believe.

Friday the 13th at 00:00

Larundel Mental Asylum

Plenty Road, Bundoora

I drop the sheet and it spirals out of control to the carpet. This is madness. Sorry for the pun, but an invitation to a mental hospital? I Google the place to find out more, and I'm left speechless. This institution was one of the last in Victoria to close. It was part of a larger complex called Mont Park. At its busiest time it housed and cared for over 750 mentally ill criminals. Criminals? Are all mentally insane people criminals? Surely not – my cousin was mad, but he wasn't a criminal. How do they determine you to be insane? Do you get a certificate? Here is your Degree of Madness. Congratulations.

I read on and find out that serial killer Peter Dupas was treated there. I wonder how well his treatment went. Police aren't sure exactly how many people he killed. Even if it's one, then that's one too many.

Despite all that, this could possibly be the single most exciting thing that will happen to me – even par with the birth of Sia.

I need to decide if I'm going … I'll shower and think about it as the hot water trickles over my body.

Be daring, Edgar. That's my real name by the way: Edgar Sanchez. *Be daring and go to this place of nutcases. You have the invite. What do you have to lose?*

And just like that, I decide to go.

Chapter 3

I get off the tram at the required stop. The streets are deserted. Strange for a Friday night in Melbourne.

An eerie feeling comes across me and does something strange to my insides. It makes the hairs on my arms stand like someone has walked over my grave. I feel nervous about this, unnaturally tense. I'm hoping the feeling will subside by the time I get in.

I'm standing in front of the building that once housed the crazies. A dead-set loony bin for the criminally insane and the clinically dead from the neck up. I'm here not knowing what to expect, but I'm willing to take that chance. I'm not usually one to dive into the deep end, but I guess you need to start sometime.

There is someone standing on the footpath. He's quite tall, with a brushy full ZZ Top beard. A long white trench coat that goes all the way down to his shins, resembling Doc from *Back to the Future*. A belt around the waist keeps the coat together.

I approach him, and before I get to him his hand is stretched out, waiting to be shaken. I put mine out and he introduces himself as Dr. Samuel Lichtenstein. Well-spoken with a slight English accent. He smells of some sort of chemical, hard to pinpoint the fragrance. Possibly aftershave. A very cheap one, at that.

He asks me for the invite. I fish it out of my jeans pocket. He unfolds it and reads it, making sure it's not a dupe. Then he passes me a nametag.

'We all need to wear one, Edgar. Here's yours.'

I take it from him and stick it onto my jumper. Then it dawns on me – how did he know my name? Did I mention it to him when he introduced himself? It wasn't on the invitation – it wasn't mine to begin with. Eager to find out, but too afraid to mention anything, I keep it quietly to myself. For now.

I realise there's another two guys. One has a nametag reading Bruce, and the other Stanley. Both are quiet and look confused. They haven't glanced my way at all. They're looking around, trying to familiarise themselves with their surroundings. Probably working out the quickest and easiest escape route, just in case they need to make a run for it.

Bruce is shorter than me, and if anyone is shorter than me then they aren't tall at all. I've been called a short-ass my whole life, but this guy takes the prize. I stand about 5'8". Bruce looks a few inches shorter. He has no facial hair; virgin smooth skin. He's wearing thick Coke bottle glasses that make his eyes look twice as big, a bit like a bug. His jacket is zipped all the way up to his neck on the verge of choking himself, and he's also wearing a dark beanie that has some logo I can't make out. Unconditionally awkward-looking.

Stanley is the opposite. He's dressed like he's ready to walk down the aisle; a dark brown or possibly black two-piece suit with a black tie. He's got blonde wavy hair like a surfer, someone you would find down at Bondi Beach – minus the suit.

We must be waiting on more to arrive. I look at my watch. It's three minutes to midnight. Three minutes before the doc calls action.

It's dead quiet out here. No one has spoken a word besides the doctor. He must have heard my thoughts – he holds up a piece of paper.

Keep quiet. Talk only when asked'.

I plan on doing that.

A car pulls up. It's an Uber. Three other people hop out, two girls and a guy. We are now six in total, seven if you count the doc.

The nametags come out again, and one by one they place them on their tops. Priya, Carmela, and Jock. *Nice to meet you,* I say in my head, remembering to keep quiet.

'It's so nice to see you all,' says the doctor. 'No need for introductions, the nametags will help you with that. How are you all feeling? Nod your head for good, shake for not.'

I nod, so does everyone else. This is so weird. It must be an experiment or something.

'At any point, if you feel anything, please bring it to my attention. Remember, no talking. You each will hold onto one of these.' He hands us a small remote-control type of buzzer. 'Whenever you feel the need to stop me, you press this button. If you get scared, press the button. If you want to quit … don't press the button, because there is no quitting. Stay close and keep your eyes peeled. I want to mention one other thing, something that will help you through this. We are safe here and nothing will happen to you physically. Just remember that. Are you ready?'

We all nod, but what did he mean by 'nothing will happen to us physically'? Will something happen mentally? It's a mental hospital, an asylum, an institution. My heart gives out a flutter and gets lost amongst all the other feelings.

'Okay. Let's go. Single file and follow me.'

The doctor leads us in.

Chapter 4

There is something familiar about the surroundings that I can't put a finger on. It's disturbing, like I know something more about this place then intended. The façade is blinking clearly in front of me. What is it about this place that I know? I push the thought aside and concentrate on the now.

We walk down the cemented path towards the entrance. Years of abandonment has caused a rift in its appearance. A spooky kind of feeling. I can sense a presence around me, like someone is going to pop out and scare the living daylights out of me.

We walk in a single file, marching into the unknown. I'm in the middle behind Priya and in front of Stanley.

It's quiet out here, aside from the occasional car that passes by on Plenty Road and the combined breathing of the group. My eyes wander from person to person. Wondering what might be going through their heads. I can tell you one thing; curiosity killed the cat and it might kill us here tonight.

The thought of how many people suffered in this place enters my head willingly. How many clinically insane people were kept medicated so they wouldn't hurt others? How many of them were ever released back out into society and returned even worse? My guess is irrelevant. We're here to see ghosts. A real ghost tour. It's like watching the movie *Ghost* all over again.

A black cat sits on its hind legs at the front double doors. The reflection of the torch bouncing off its beady eyes makes them glow in the dark like a lava lamp. Its ears prick up, sensing that humans are approaching. It takes cover through the broken glass panel on the door and runs into the building. There must be more stray cats in there, something to be wary of. I make a mental note of it in case one jumps out and tries scaring me.

Mental note. I laugh at my thought.

The door is padlocked with a long chain. Not sure whether they're trying to keep people out, or people in. Now that's a thought for the sane.

Dr. Samuel reaches for a key on his lanyard and unlocks the padlock. The key goes directly back around his neck. The creak from the glass panelled door echoes when the doors are opened. A noise reaches us from the dimly-lit corridor.

I feel that déjà vu creep in again – I've seen this place somewhere before. Snippets of memory coming back. I've seen this corridor … maybe from a photo in a book, or online? Or maybe in a brochure. But my memory isn't giving anything away, yet.

The last of the group squeeze through the door. We're filed in and grouped together in the foyer. The front desk sits unattended in front of us. Pictures of what it used to look like flash in front of me. No one has spoken since we began the tour, no one dares. Buzzers have replaced our voice boxes. Our eyes and ears are the main functional organs.

The air is thick inside this place. Hard to breathe, and making swallowing difficult. I catch movement from the side of my eye. False alarm; it's just the others who are with me. My imagination kicks in and I notice a short, overweight lady behind the desk holding a clipboard. She makes her way over to us. Her hair is tied in a bun. Her uniform is so tight, it makes her stomach hang over the edge of her belt.

I look closer and notice a resemblance – she looks so much like the lady in the blue uniform from the café. Surely it can't be her. I'll just play along with it and see where it leads.

She introduces herself as Sarah Guinness, like the beer. I thought she had said, 'Share a Guinness.' Funny how the mind works and what your ears think they hear. 'Yes, please,' would have been my answer.

The words and her appearance are faint, like a hologram. *This is a bloody good show*, I think to myself. Even if the characters aren't real, the lighting makes it look unbelievable. The others seem to be mesmerised with what she is saying. I don't catch that much of the conversation; their expressions are more eye-catching, their intensity.

Dr. Samuel is staring at us. I wonder what could be going through his mind. He has a half-smile on his face, enjoying what he's witnessing.

'Share a Guinness' raises her hand and points towards Bruce. She signals for him to follow her. I look around and watch him push his way through the group, brushing shoulders with a few of them. He follows her down the corridor. Isn't anyone going to stop him? *Dr. Samuel, stop Bruce from following the ghost!* I need to say something. I can't hold it in any longer.

'Bruce!'

Sarah turns her head and glances back towards me, knowing it was me who spoke. She lifts her index finger to her mouth and presses it against her closed lips.

'Shh.'

The sound came out louder than I had thought I would hear it. It was so loud, as if she was really here with us.

She leads Bruce into the first room, just past the desk. The rooms are positioned adjacent to one another down the corridor. We follow them to the entrance of the room. There is a name on the door.

BRUCE O'BRIAN

Okay, I'm freaking out now. What kind of ghost tour is this where people's names are appearing on doors? Is Bruce an actor and part of the show? Whatever is going on, it's confusing the hell out of me.

Bruce takes a seat on the bed. Two other guys are in there with him, both in light blue uniforms. Bruce removes his shirt. They attach wires using tape to his hairy chest. He turns and faces the wall, exposing his back to us. There are two large black burn marks on his lower back that look like they could have been made by an iron. He looks over to where we're standing and gives us a smile, an indication that he's going to be okay.

One of the guys walks over to the machine that the wires are attached to and flicks it on. A volt of electricity pulses through the wires and penetrates the top layer of Bruce's skin. He screams.

What are they doing to him? He looks like he's in so much unbearable pain and discomfort.

Sarah closes the door, muffling the noise until only the sound of meowing is heard. The black cat? I assume it's the same cat. I look over Jock's shoulder and notice that the cat is walking slowly towards the other rooms.

Everyone turns and begins to follow the cat. I stay a few steps behind. I want to see what has happened to Bruce. I'm curious to know why they would do that. Why they would shock him and then leave him behind?

Curiosity gets the better of me.

Trying not to make a sound, I turn the handle. The door opens with ease. The room is empty. No bed, no machine, no Bruce.

I feel like it was all a dream, my imagination. I close the door and move along the corridor, catching up with the others. I keep it to myself. No questions asked.

Chapter 5

I'm still trying to understand what happened to Bruce. I still can't believe that nobody out of the group did anything to stop it, especially Dr. Samuel. Did it really happen or was it my imagination?

We all follow along the marked path, I can almost see the footprints that were made by the lunatics before this place was closed down. I wonder if Peter Dupas was housed in this section? I should have read up more about him. I might do that when I get home later on this morning. I had forgotten to ask when I arrived here how long this tour will go for. Normally, tours like this would go for a few hours, at least.

This room opposite to where Bruce was has the blinds drawn and the door shut. There is a light coming from under the door. I didn't think this place still ran electricity. I assumed it had been cut when the institution closed down years ago. Maybe they have a generator running for tours to make it as realistic as possible. Trapdoors in the walls for the actors to appear and disappear through, cameras to film all the guests getting scared out of their boots. Well planned and orchestrated.

Dr. Samuel stops and speaks to us in a soft tone. He sounds a little like my doctor; Dr. Ross has a very similar tone and sound. He speaks with comfort and reassurance. I wonder if they know each other. Dr. Ross worked in an institution many years ago before he became a family GP. So many similarities.

'Can anyone picture what this room might look like in your minds?'

Odd question, I thought, *seeing no one has ever been here before.* Maybe there is something online about it? I feel for my phone in my pocket. It's not there. I must have left it at home. I wish I'd stop forgetting things.

I see a hand go up. I don't remember her name; she is a pretty girl, with a tattoo of a swastika on her neck. I try and read her nametag but she's standing at an awkward angle, her back exposed more than her front. She turns enough for me to get a quick glance at it. Carmela. She must have a strong liking for the Nazis.

'Yes, I thought you would have known, Carmela. This is something you would have experienced in your time. Do you remember much about it?'

She nods. She must have read an article about this room. I wonder if she knows which patient was stationed in this room? I need to know. I lower my voice and speak over the doctor, but low enough for only Carmela to hear me.

'What site did you read this on?'

She doesn't even flinch. Like she hadn't even heard me, or most likely ignored what I've said. I know we're not meant to talk, but that is plain rude. Should I ask again? I might get the same response. Fuck it. I don't need to know right away. I'll do my own research and look it up later.

The door to the room opens and Sarah appears right in front of us.

'Oh shit,' I say. 'Where did you come from?'

Her finger goes to her lips again. I know what's coming.

'Shh.'

She walks over and places her hand on Carmela's shoulder. This will be fun. What surprises are planned for her? The electric shock has already been used. From behind me I hear a racket. Screams coming from around the corner that are getting louder. What the fuck is happening?

I look behind me and I see a group of women running frantically towards us. The women are dressed in blue uniforms. They must be nurses or orderlies, or possibly a posse of crazed inmates. Everything is happening way too fast for me; my mind can't keep up.

I back up and plant myself firmly up against the wall, trying to keep out of their way. I have no desire to get bowled over. The doctor and the rest of the group do the same. All but Carmela. All eyes are on her.

To my surprise, she begins to sprint away from the angry mob. Before the runners get to us, another group of three ladies run out of the room. They're dressed like patients. They take off after Carmela. This scene is getting way too weird for me now. I don't know who is chasing who and why. It's like a scene from Benny Hill. Fast forward has been pushed on the remote and everything starts fading out of focus. I listen out for chase music to top things off. Sound effects would be so awesome right now.

My back is up against the wall, hands flat behind my back, trying to separate myself from lurking danger. I'll admit, I'm scared shitless. Scared something will happen. Scared I'm not going to make it out of here, alive.

I close my eyes really tight and keep them closed for a long time. Afraid to open them, afraid to witness what is going down. Danger right in front of me. I keep repeating to myself that *I'll be okay, I'll be okay, I'll be okay. I WILL BE OKAY.*

I open my eyes slowly.

I'm no longer here. I've been transported somewhere else, somewhere my mind has never taken me before. I'm still in the institute, only now the scene looks different. I'm leaning up against the wall, overlooking the chaos that is happening in front of me.

An alarm is blasting loudly from the overhead speakers, nestled in the corners of the ceiling. Everything around me is painted a bright happy colour. Only it isn't a happy time. I'm still scared.

The orderlies move past me at speed. They must still be following Carmela. Are they trying to stop her from doing something? I need to follow them to find out, but my legs won't carry me. They feel glued to the tiled floor. Everything around me is moving at super speed and I'm getting dizzy. I can't keep up. I need this to stop.

I yell as loud as I can, but nothing comes out. My mouth is open and I feel myself yelling but I can't hear anything. I realise I am wearing a mask. My breathing is heavy and muffled. I'm taking extra breaths to stay alive.

I remove my mask and move on with my mission. Why is Carmela running?

I turn the corner and see her. She's cornered by a man. I see a large blade. The reflection from the knife blinding me. It's like staring directly into the sun. I don't know the guy holding the knife. He looks somewhat familiar though. Could it be Peter, the serial killer? I need to stop him, no matter who it is.

I approach them in stealthy movements. They don't know I'm there.

Then he does the unthinkable … but at the same time, it's what murderers do. He stabs her repeatedly in the stomach, a frenzied attack.

I step back slowly, trying not to make myself known to them. I don't want to be the next victim. Witnesses usually die in situations like these. The alarm is whooping loudly and a voice over the PA is yelling about a Code Black. Doctors come from every direction.

It's too late. Her body is on the floor convulsing, running out of breath. Blood pouring out like a water fountain. The floor is turning red. The knife bandit is standing over her in victory. Blood drips from the tip of the knife. I still can't see who the person is. I don't think I want to know.

I back up around the corner and I'm back to where I started from. The scene has turned back to the present.

Dr. Samuel is standing there with a concerned look. Stanley, Priya, and Jock glance my way but don't make eye contact. Carmela is missing.

My heart is thumping faster than a racehorse after a victorious run.

My mind is travelling quicker then lightning. Visions of the past have flashed before me. I saw Carmela get butchered. She suffered a horrible death. I was there, but didn't do anything about it. What could I have done?

But I couldn't have been there – I'm here, now. My mind is scrambled. I need to get out of here, but Dr. Samuel said there is no quitting. I need to see it out.

Please be over soon.

Chapter 6

I always allocate myself time to collect my thoughts and recuperate between classes. Unfortunately, I don't have the luxury of doing that right now. Everything is moving way too fast for my liking, making me feel like I'm in a silent movie; me being the one always looking surprised.

The evening started with excitement, but now I just want this to end. I want to go home. Something is happening here that I cannot understand and, to be honest, I don't want to. I want to ask for a timeout but I know all too well that that is not possible. Clear instructions were handed out before we began. No quitting.

I won't be quitting, though. I just need a little time to get my head around it. It's not fucking making any sense. A timeout is not quitting.

We turn right, away from where the action had just unfolded a minute ago, and head for what seems to have been the cafeteria when this dingy place was operating. Too afraid to look to my left, I focus on walking straight, eyes to the right, hoping I don't run into anything.

But something is drawing me to look over my shoulder. I don't want to but I do. Five minutes ago, Carmela was lying dead on the floor opposite us. Now there is nothing there, not even a body.

I'm glad the body is gone, actually taken away. I didn't want to see her like that again. It's fucking with my head and my innocence is fading into nothing. Maybe I never had any innocence? Maybe I have always been this way and had never noticed? But I'm a teacher. Surely, they can see that I'm sane, right? Not the insane teacher teaching the insane students.

Come to think of it, not many people pay much attention to me when I'm present. My students make out like I'm not even there. I've questioned them and I get the same response – nothing. At least they hand in all their work. It could be worse. I've even brought it up with Mr. Kluger. 'Like it or leave it,' he says to me. More days than not I try to convince myself I should leave teaching altogether. Do something else, something that will stimulate my mind in a different way. I definitely don't like teaching.

We approach the cafeteria. Everything seems to have been left as it was the day they decided to close this place down. Tables and chairs fill up the empty seating area. Cloths cover the furniture to protect it from dust. I once read somewhere that dust is 70% dried skin cells. Can you imagine that? We are breathing in dead human skin particles, digesting it into our system with the rest of the crap that makes up dust.

Gross.

Then you have these health freaks who tell you, 'Don't eat this,' or 'Don't drink that because it's bad for you, it might kill you one day.' Um, hello? You're swallowing dead skin, you morons. Might as well eat someone – you might even get nutrition from it. Bring back cannibalism, I say. Actually, some countries still have it.

Just a thought.

We pull the sheets off the chairs and take a break. We sit there in silence. The group is getting smaller the longer we go on. Priya keeps looking at me like she knows me, or she fancies me. I'm quite sure I don't know who she is. I've never seen her in my life. I've never seen any of these people before. Just like this experience, they are all new to me. She looks over and smiles again. Is she flirting with me? It's been a while. I forget what flirting feels like. Since my wife left me many years ago, I haven't been on a date or out to dinner with friends. I haven't spoken to another woman. Believe me when I say I only had eyes for one woman. Now that she's gone, well, I don't really see the point or have the desire to have what's second best.

Do I still love Stella? That's my ex-wife, the mother of our child, the causer of grief and the pain in my ass. Obviously, I don't tell her that. She can get a little fiery sometimes. Actually, all the time.

But yes, I do.

Dr. Samuel takes his backpack off and places it on the table. I didn't even realise he was wearing one. I normally pay more attention to detail. I'm not sure how I missed this one.

He unzips it and digs deep to pull out a plastic bag. The bag itself has something in it. Choc-coated muesli bars. He hands us each one. I notice he has enough bars, the exact amount for whoever is left. There should be two more bars – one for Bruce and one for Carmela – but the bag is empty.

I speak before I think. I seem to always open my trap at all the wrong times. 'You should have two more muesli bars, Dr. Samuel.'

He looks over and smiles. At this moment, I feel like I'm the student and he the teacher, and I'm about to get into trouble for saying something so stupid.

'I think you have it wrong there, Mr. Sanchez. If you look closely, everyone has a bar. I brought the right amount.'

'But what about the other two?'

'What other two, Edgar?'

'Bruce and Carmela.'

'There was no Bruce and Carmela.'

I have to stop talking because none of this makes any sense. I saw the other two with my own eyes. We started this tour together. They vanished during the first part and haven't returned. I saw their nametags that clearly read Bruce and Carmela. I'm not blind. We had another two people on this tour and now there is no trace of them.

He continues speaking and it all comes out like crazy talk. The longer he speaks, the more he's sounding like my GP.

'Bruce and Carmela were never here with us. You must be mistaking this for another time in your life when you knew a Bruce and a Carmela. Could that be what is going on here?'

I look around for something to drink. Water would be nice. My mouth is dry and my brain is sizzling. I need to stay focused or I will lose my mind. Dr. Samuel is making no sense at all. I've been off the grog for years before two nights ago. It had done something to my mental health the last time I drank. Not sure what, but I didn't feel well after it. It made me sick to the point I had thrown up so much it felt like my insides had come out with it. I spent some time locked up to recover. I remember lying on a hard metal bed that was so uncomfortable. I haven't had a drink since. Well, you know what I mean.

I've eaten half the muesli bar. Something about it tastes off. I look for the wrapper to see if the date has expired, but the wrapper is gone. Did they give me the bar without the wrapper? I can't remember.

I put the remaining half-eaten bar in my pocket, making out I've eaten the whole thing. My mouth is beginning to feel funny and unhappy. My lips are stinging and my cheeks feel like they've grown. I'm having a hard time breathing. Sweat has made its way to the surface of my skin. My forehead is dripping with it, as if I've done hours of running. My mind is the only thing untouched.

A memory is resurfacing as I'm beginning to stress. Dr. Samuel has given us something to activate it. He must have injected the bar with memory juice or something. He's an evil doctor. I've known a few in my life. Wait, what? How do I remember that? I had an evil doctor? What the fuck is happening?

The sweat flows more profusely as time continues on. Everyone around me is moving in waves. I glance at Dr. Samuel. He's the only one who looks steady, the only one I can make out, the only one that's not moving. The others are just pulsating lines.

The cafeteria is coming to life. Colour appears, and the noise is deafening. People talking, machines operating, even the drinks fridge is on. I can see cold water bottles in there ready to be drunk.

Someone taps me on my shoulder. It's Sarah. She's standing there with the knife that was used to kill Carmela. The sharp pointy blade is inches from my nose. I can smell the metallic scent of blood. Carmela's blood.

I move my head back a few inches to separate me from the blade. It works. I can't smell it anymore. I look at the blade again. It's clean now. Someone has cleaned the blood off it. But how? I've been staring at it this entire time.

I jump. Someone has pricked my arm with something. A needle? I look at my arm. My top is off and there is a trickle of blood coming out of a tiny pinprick. My heart starts beating faster and harder. It has a rhythm I'm familiar with. A sad song I have heard many times.

The last time I heard this song was at a funeral. Who's funeral? I know. I remember whose funeral it was.

I put my hand up to my mouth and cover it so I don't scream.

The funeral I heard this song at was Carmela's.

I pass out.

Chapter 7

I open my eyes. Fragments of my memory appear in dribs and drabs. I'm in a white room. Am I dead? I don't feel dead, but then what does death feel like? I'll never know.

The room is so bright it hurts my eyes. I look around and notice there aren't any windows. Is it still night outside? Have I dreamt the whole thing? It feels like a dream. I've dreamt of some crazy shit before. This is the closest any of my dreams that have come to reality.

I remember every detail of this dream. The invitation, the blue uniform lady, the doctor. Poor Carmela. She died in my dream. I wonder who she really was? Whether she had family? She must have, everyone has one. I should look her up once I'm out of here. I don't know her surname, though. That's okay, Google has all the answers – I'll ask them. The best free information around.

The door opens. I can see beyond the entrance. It's also white. Not like my room though, it's a never-ending distant white. It goes on and on. Maybe there are stairs that lead to heaven? Maybe I am dead. It could be a sign. I should check it out.

I try to remove the covers but notice I'm in restraints. Why have they strapped me down onto this bed? I try to wiggle free but I can't move. The straps are secured tightly. I call for help. The echo bounces off all the walls and comes back at me like a cry for forgiveness.

I hear a muffled conversation coming from outside my room. I can't tell who's out there, I don't recognise the voice. I call out again but this time I tone it down a notch.

'Hello?' A little friendlier.

Dr. Samuel walks in. It's so nice to see a familiar face. He'll know what is happening. He'll know why I'm in here. He breaks the silence in the room.

'Hello, Edgar. How are you feeling today?'

Today? How long have I been here? It was evening the last time my eyes were open.

'Doc, what's going on?'

'You overreacted and needed time to calm down. You got a little worked up and agitated with what someone had said.'

'So why am I tied to a bed?'

'It's for your own safety, Edgar. And those around you.'

'What do you mean, safety? We're on a tour, Dr. Samuel. Safety from what? Ghosts?'

Sarah comes in holding a syringe. She passes it to Dr. Samuel. He rolls up my sleeve and jabs me with it. It feels like ice running through my veins. I get cold and my eyes become heavy. What has he given me?

'I'll be back in a little while. I'll give you time to rest. Sleep well, Edgar.'

'Doc, wait, please tell me what is hap…'

That was all I could muster. Someone has turned the volume down. My heartbeat is all I can hear. I need to get out of here, NOW.

They both leave. The room is now clear. My mind and body are still functioning. I try to move my legs. I feel them move. I need to see how much strength I have in me before this drug they have given me fully kicks in. My fingers move to the beat of my heart. I muster all the strength I have and push upwards towards the restraints. There is a lot more movement in them than I had initially expected. I take a deep breath and hold it in for a few seconds before I push up hard, with everything I have in me, and let out a huge roar. The belts come loose and break free from the bed. I feel free. My body jolts upright and I leap out of bed.

And then I'm back at the cafeteria with Dr. Samuel and the others. It's quite dark in there. The reflection of the moon is projecting from a broken skylight. The noise is dimmed; no people talking, no noise from coffee machines and no noise from the drinks vending machine.

I look around to see if Sarah is there with the knife. She's gone, too.

My memory had taken me back to something that had happened. I don't remember when that was, though. I must have read it somewhere, like most things that have happened here tonight. Whatever it was, it fucking scared me. I'm glad I'm back now. I feel safe again, but the sweat stains under my armpits tell another story. It was as real as it felt.

Chapter 8

I had hoped for an exciting evening, but what I'm getting is more than I can chew. If tonight was to be my last, then I can definitely say I went out with a bang.

Why am I the only one talking? The doctor acknowledges my presence, but none of the others have said a word. It's like they're not even here. Jock is pacing up and down like a caged beast, counting, looking overly nervous with every step he takes. I had a cousin who did that. He was later diagnosed with autism. He still does it, twenty years later. Jock stops and looks up. He locks eyes with something that's not there. He looks over at us and for a split second I think he's about to say something.

Dr. Samuel pulls out a folder from his bag. He opens it and hands us each a piece of paper. I read mine and look at the others. They hand theirs back to the doctor. I read it once more and hand it back to him.

'Edgar, you hold onto yours. Yours is different to the others.'

'What makes mine different?'

'You'll see when the time is right.'

I want to believe him but I'm having a difficult time believing anything right now. I guess I have to wait. I just want to get out of here unscathed.

Jock takes off, wandering towards the west wing corridor. It's darker down there. We all stand and follow Jock. We used to play a game called Follow the Leader when I was a kid. It was so much fun. I remember never wanting to lead for some reason. Now Jock is our leader and we follow him.

There are no rooms at the first section but there is a large room at the end. A large wooden door separates us from the other side.

I've never spoken about ghosts or the supernatural to anyone. I've watched an abundance of movies about them, but never spoke about it openly. Not many people believe in it anyway. 'How much of it is real?' they say. 'Probably all of it,' is what I want to say.

The wooden door opens and stays open. A cold chilled breeze enters through the open door, ruffling the papers on the walls. My hair is quite long, and the wind is blowing it to one side. It reminds me that I need a haircut. My hairdresser only works Saturdays. Today will be perfect. I'll walk in and wait if I have to.

Jock walks through the door, and we follow. It leads out to a courtyard. I look up to the skies. Clouds cover the night sky. I can smell rain in the air. The wind has picked up from the time we arrived here.

The yard is large. There must have been benches here once upon a time, but now there is only fallen leaves and broken branches from the overhead trees. The sound of rustling dried leaves swirling around like a miniature tornado.

Flood lights come on in the courtyard, like Centre Court at Rod Laver Arena – Jock in his Grand Slam final. He stops and drops to his knees, both hands out in front of him, staring directly towards the soil. He raises his head towards God up above. He looks like he's about to lie down, begging for something that will save him from this present moment.

Sarah arrives holding a tray with something on it. It's not clear from where I'm standing but they look like surgical instruments. Jock looks over, and his eyes focus on the tray. His eyes are glowing with tears, guilt and sadness.

Behind me a phone starts ringing. There is a payphone just outside the door. I hadn't noticed it there when I came out. It's rung about three times and no one has moved to answer it. Someone needs to pick it up. Sarah does just that.

'Hello Mrs. McKenzie. I'm sorry, but Jock is dead. He didn't survive the operation. We did everything we could. Bye for now. God bless.'

A bolt of lightning sparkles in the distant sky. Thunder will surely follow. I look around for cover. We should head in before it starts raining.

I look back over at Jock. He's lying flat on his back with a white sheet covering him from head to toe. There's a red bloodstain around his midsection.

'Isn't anyone going to help him?' My words land on deaf ears. Why isn't anyone listening to me?

'Hello, are you listening?' I ask, angry now. 'Why isn't anyone helping?'

Two orderlies exit from the wooden door holding one of those old-fashioned army stretchers you see on *M*A*S*H*. I'm waiting for Hawkeye and B.J. Hunnicutt to appear and try to patch him up.

I watch them leave through the wooden door. The red phone box is no longer there. It's like *The Twilight Zone* – things appear then disappear right in front of your eyes. I need to escape from this tormented, mind-controlled situation I'm experiencing. It's way too fucked up to even think about.

I have a plan. They know me by name, but not where I live. Once they head off, I'll hang back behind the pack and make a run for it. I can hear the cars passing in the distance. Plenty Road must not be that far from where I'm standing. I know the direction I need to run. I won't let anything stop me.

What is left of the posse follow Dr. Samuel back inside. My feet are planted flat on the ground, ready for my grand escape. They can try and chase me but I know I'm faster. I was a track and field athlete at school and my slender body and short powerful legs never forgot how to run and jump. Half marathons and fun runs have been my favourite activities over the past twenty years.

The group makes their way back in through the wooden doors. Once they are out of sight I scoot for the nearest shrub. I'll lay low for a few minutes. I look through the branches and keep myself well hidden. Easier than I thought.

The coast is clear. This is my opportunity to leave. But there is a figure in the exit path. Sarah is standing between me and my escape. I need to distract her. I pick up a branch and throw it in the opposite direction from where she is looking, just like in the movies. She looks over to where the noise generates her attention. I can't believe it actually worked. Now is my chance.

I spring up, leap over the bush, and head towards the opening. I run like the wind, like my life depends on it – which it does. I'm in the clear from any danger. Sarah hasn't even noticed me.

I'm around the corner, heading for Plenty Road. I get there in time to meet the tram at its stop. What luck! I hop on and crouch down so as not to be seen. The doors close and the tram begins to move. I'm out of there and heading home. My haven, my safety.

The ride takes about twenty minutes. It drops me off two blocks from home. I walk in darkness through the streets of Preston. It's quiet and the weather is beginning to break. Droplets of rain hit my bare skin. I make it home before the heavens open up and pours its tears of joy down upon me.

I take out my keys and unlock the door. The familiar smell of my flat brings comfort to my nose. The sound of the filter in the fish tank doing its thing. I should buy some fish to go in there. It will look prettier.

I take my shoes off at the front entrance and feel that my socks are wet. How is that possible? Possibly from running through the high grass. It could have been wet.

I run the water in the shower, extra hot. It leaves red blotchy marks on my chest. Almost at boiling point, but bearable. I stand there with my head under the water, thinking back over the evening that had unfolded before my eyes. Trying to make sense of the senseless. My mind feels unconscious.

The shower lasts twelve minutes. The longest I have ever been in here. I dry myself and hop into my PJs. I look around for my phone, but I can't see it anywhere. I've misplaced it and can't remember where I'd put it. It could be on charge in my room. I head out there when there's a knock at the door. I look at the clock on the wall. 4:13am Saturday morning. Melbourne is still asleep at this hour, yet someone is knocking on my door.

I put my robe on and make my way there. I wait for them to knock again but they don't. I open the door to find no one there. A yellow envelope sits neatly on my front doorstep. It's sealed with nothing on it besides my full name in black Sharpie.

I look down the spiral steps towards the front of the building. All clear besides a bike chained to the railings that belongs to the man in Number Six. I pick up the envelope and close the door. It feels heavy. I make my way to the kitchen and sit at the table. I move the fruit bowl out of the way to give myself some space. I stare at it for a minute before attempting to open it. It's stuck together well; tape overlapping the sticky seal. I rip it open with some force.

I pour the contents out to find documents and newspaper clippings. I start reading the documents. They don't make any sense. It's about former patients at Larundel Mental Asylum. I read the first page and leave the rest to ponder.

My interest is in the clippings. I pick up the first one. The article is about a fire that broke out in the kitchen. They believe it was deliberately lit as a distraction. It also says that two patients plus three staff were killed in the blaze. The rest of the patients and staff were evacuated to the courtyard behind the cafeteria. There is a picture above the story. There is a person lying on the ground with a sheet that's covering him. He's dead. Two orderlies standing next to the body with a group of people in the background.

I look closer to the group in the background. I see two familiar faces. Priya and Stanley. They were there at the institution when the fire occurred. Maybe that's why they were there tonight. They wanted to get in touch with the spirits of the people who perished. It all makes sense now. I read on to find out more.

Family and friends are mourning the death of Jock McKenzie who was tragically killed today in a wild attack. Mr. McKenzie was pronounced dead at the scene. He is the third person to have fallen victim to the madman who went on a sadistic, calculated rampage. The person responsible for the murders is—

Damn. Someone has ripped off the part that mentions the name. Who was it? I'll get back to it. There might be something in the other clippings.

I pick up another one. This one is larger and seems to be full of information. There is a photo. I try and look at it but my vision is a little blurry. My eyes adjust. The photo is now clear.

My heart stops. My life as I knew it has just ended. I stand and my fingers lose grip of the clipping. It glides to the floor and rests at my feet.

What I read makes me hold my breath. I don't want to ever breathe again.

Chapter 9

An iconic and controversial building in Mont Park has closed its doors for the final time.

Larundel Mental Asylum, originally built in the 1930s, has recently been under scrutiny due to the high demand of patients who have recently 'run loose and wild'. The final straw was drawn three weeks ago when a long serving patient went on a rampage, setting fire to the kitchen in the cafeteria and killing two staff and three patients.

The victims were identified as Patrick Hako, 32, Head Psychiatric Nurse Sarah Guinness, 56, and patients Philip Cardamone, Jock McKenzie, and Carmela Vialli.

Dr. Samuel Lichtenstein told police that this was a tragic ordeal that had lasted over an hour.

'We had the patient on trial medication that has a great track record in Germany. The number of patients that have stabilised and improved using this drug has proven its affect. Trials began here in January last year and saw a dramatic drop in anger managed patients. This was a carefully orchestrated attack that had been on the books for ages. We found the diary that was kept under his mattress. None of us saw it coming. Our sympathies go to all the victims' families and friends who are affected by this.'

Dr. Lichtenstein went public with the drug that was used and the affect it had. He had praised it and recommended it to all institutions.

The perpetrator was later cornered and forced police to take action after lunging at them with a large kitchen knife before he was gunned down. He died at the scene. He was identified as 44-year old Edgar Louis Sanchez of Preston.

THE WEDDING

Chapter 1

20 January 2023

How far would you go to make someone's life a misery, a living Hell? Someone you've known for almost your entire life. Someone you hold close to your heart for all the wrong reasons.

I know how far I'd go.

The story I'm about to tell begins with me planning the ultimate end, a year or thereabouts in the making. The sleepless nights staying up late, thinking of the worst things I could possibly do to her. I won't lie; I've considered murder. Who hasn't in the situation I'm in? It's up there with all the other sinister ideas that have been born in my head. One single spark has created this monster within me.

The truth is, that monster has always been there, hidden so deep in my thoughts that it only appears when cornered; when no one else is around to experience the pleasure of this demon. It even scares me to the point of uncontrollable nightmares. Trust me, I know about nightmares.

Since it has always been there, it just needed that nudge; that push to be dislodged from the darkest and cruellest place inside my head. Now that it's freed, it won't leave until the job is completed.

I have been waiting for the invitation. To the wedding. I know I've been invited because a friend saw my name on the guestlist.

I was really hoping to get invited. I wanted to be there, to see this unfold. To watch Suzi Dawson's face change from happiness to horror. This wedding will be one the guests won't ever forget. I'll make sure of that.

I'm standing downstairs in front of the lounge room window. The silky sheer curtains are open. I have a clear view to the letterbox, and my eyes focus on the people walking by. I'm waiting for that person with the yellow high-vis vest and khaki pants, holding his satchel full of letters. My invitation is in that bag.

I also know it's going to be delivered today because my friend received theirs yesterday. They live two blocks away. They usually get their letters a day before I do. I'm so excited. I am trying hard to contain the jubilation that is building up inside my stomach. Butterflies the size of birds.

I have a Plan B, just in case Plan A goes to shit. You should always have a plan B. Sometimes even a C – in case you're really desperate. At this point, I'm confident with Plans A and B.

The houses around here are quiet at this time of the morning. Most of the neighbourhood is at work or school. I'm meant to be at work but swapped my shift with Tiana, who loves doing the morning shift. I would have done anything to give me the day off so I can wait for my prized package.

I wait for over half an hour. I should have made my coffee earlier. I get nervous and coffee is the only thing that calms me. I'll only be gone maybe four minutes … fuck it. I decide to go.

The machine can get loud sometimes and Mum is asleep upstairs. It shouldn't wake her. She's been sleeping longer these days. Her cancer is getting worse and she's lost heaps of weight. She's what they call 'skin and bone', and is starting to look like someone suffering through a famine. She spends more and more days lying in bed until she gets so cramped she struggles to move.

I make her a coffee, too. That's all she drinks these days – coffee and Baileys. Maybe because they look alike, same colour and shit. Probably even have the same effect. Who knows?

The machine is ready in no time. Cups out and sugar loaded. One sugar for me and three for Mum. I know what you're thinking – that much sugar is going to kill her, eventually. But she's dying anyway. Why not die happy?

Don't judge me, I know you are. I bet there are many who think like I do. Many.

So fuck you.

If I take the coffee up to her right away, I shouldn't be more than 45 seconds – plenty of time to get back down in position. I'll time myself so I know for next time.

Oh, wait. There will be no next time. If this plan works, then next time will be just a thought. I blame my OCD for this, but that's our secret. Not even Mum knows I suffer from one of many disorders. She thinks I'm this normal person with a bright future ahead of me.

She's not wrong. As long as I don't get caught, which I won't because my plan is bullet-proof, like the unsinkable ship, my future looks bright. Up there with the stars like Jeffrey Dahmer and Ted Bundy.

Yes, I know many criminals think the same. But the difference is, I'm not a criminal. I'm someone who just wants revenge. I'm seeing the big picture here and in it I win. In my pictures I never lose. Ever.

Does that make me evil? Of course not.

Well, maybe just a little.

I love the way I think.

Coffee is delivered in thirty-seven seconds. I normally stay and chat to Mum. She forgets a lot and she repeats herself often. Early stages of Alzheimer's. She forgets she's dying from cancer some days. That really sucks.

This time I just drop the coffee off and leave.

I return to my post by the window and wait. I start feeling anxious. Anxiety, another one of those things I suffer from. Another thing no one knows about besides my doctor. I blame school and my upbringing for all these problems I'm experiencing now.

I pee a bit in my pants. He's arrived on time, the postman! The yellow vest stands out from the colourful beds of roses. We have red and orange, some whites and pinks, but the one prettiest right at this moment is the yellow one.

He reaches into his bag and pulls out a handful of letters. I clearly see it in his hand, it stands out from the rest. A large turquoise envelope. It's larger than the rest of the mail. He has to bend it slightly for it to fit in the mailbox. I would normally care, but not today. Today I want to rip that shit open and see the contents, see my name on that invitation. I don't give a fuck if it's bent. I'm not planning on keeping the invitation at the end.

Actually, maybe I should. Have it framed and placed on my bedside table. A memory to come back to.

My hands shake — psychotic spasms, trembling with fear — or is it excitement? I'm leaning more towards excitement.

The postman lifts his head and focuses on the next house. He rides off with his left sock pulled up over his pant leg like a school kid, not realising that the letter he has just dropped off to me will change the course of a few people's lives. Rewrite their future. Not mine, but someone else's.

I make my way outside. The air is not cold, just crisp. There's residue on the concrete path from the rain the previous night. The sun is up early this morning; my guess is that it should be dry by lunchtime. As I reach the letterbox, I feel like I'm standing in front of the Mona Lisa, about to reach into her gut and pull out the Holy Grail of invites.

The letters feel warm in my hand. My vision blurs until I get to the invitation. This beautiful piece of paperwork. My doing, of course.

I walk back in so as not to be spotted by Mrs. Angelopoulos from next door. The nosey old Greek fart can't keep to herself. One of these days I might have to smother her with her own pillow while she's having a nana nap.

Once inside, I leave the letters that mean nothing to me on the front entrance table to be opened later. There is only one with my name on it. The one in my hand. The one that means the most to me.

Mum calls me from upstairs. I need to go for now.

Chapter 2

For as long as anyone from the clan can remember it had always been about Suzi and Anthony through high school. These two were like a king and queen, Sonny and Cher, Bonnie and Clyde. Everyone wanted to be like them. All the girls wanted to be in Suzi's Bitches Club while the boys hung out just to be close to Anthony's Dirt Bags.

Obviously, it wasn't anything like Rydell High from *Grease*, and Suzi and Anthony were no Sandy and Danny, but these two were as close as you could get. Suzi had that long blonde hair every guy dreamt of on a girl, with streaks of brown and copper running through it which made her look different to Barbie. Her face, on the other hand, could have been used to mould a Barbie doll. She had a body that would bring a marathon to a stand-still; breasts that perked at the right size and angle and an ass that went *pow*. Perfect from head to toe.

Anthony was as evenly and perfectly manufactured. Tall and broad enough to be a full-back, height and size he had inherited from his grandfather. A chiselled jawline that Max Headroom made famous in the 80s. Straight white teeth that had the Macleans sparkle and a six-pack you won't find in a bottle shop.

These two were made to order; priceless.

The names of their two groups were made up by the ones who couldn't get in. Outsiders who stood no chance of joining these two possies. Only the elite could get a look – you had to be a loyal prick or a cunning mole. If you were part of the clique, then you were safe – safe from abuse, physically and mentally.

Their friends would always joke that 'once you've been touched by Anthony, you'll have The McCollough Effect.' A phenomenon of human visual perception. Look it up, it's pretty awesome. Like it or not, somehow you would always see it their way.

As the years went by, each member of the posse had grown into a respectful adult. People generally change – some for the better, others for the worse. The haters had become the forgivers and the wannabes had become close mates. That's evolution we've all become accustomed to. A hefty price they paid back at school.

Ten years after graduating, the lovebirds are finally tying the knot. Some would love to see the knot tied around their necks. You could say they both have their haters. In ten months' time, Suzi and Anthony will become Mr. and Mrs. McCollough.

The invites to the wedding went out last week. Suzi received hers today – she wanted to feel special and mailed one to herself. One would say that's pretty special.

She had received a recommendation a while ago from a friend for an invitation printer. Inspired By Design is a little firm nestled amongst the bustling metropolis of Fitzroy Street, Brunswick. It was recommended by her high school mate, Julie, and what a great suggestion it was. The invitations are amazing – just as Suzi had imagined. Detailed to perfection. *This will be the best wedding anyone has ever been to,* she thinks.

The day Suzi had ordered the invitations, her bestie Betty was with her. They are the conjoined twins, attached at the hip and sharing the same brain. There might be some rare occasions where you won't see them together, but you can count those times on one hand. People who didn't know them would swear they had come out of the same mother.

They also met up with Elizabeth, also known as Barti, that day. She had taken the day off from work and was planning on having lunch with her mother. Taking time off from work is not as easy for her as the other two girls. Come to think of it, the other two are never at work. It pays to be living at home with Mum and Dad, living off their cash and borrowed time. Things will change after the wedding for Suzi, though. She'll have new commitments to contend with that come hand in hand with a thing called 'marriage', the beginning of a new life.

Before entering the printers, the girls duck into the café next door called Don't Be Latte, which serves the nicest soy latte in town. These girls are not short of attitude, but they take fussiness to another level. The café needs to be up to their standards. If it's not, then social media get to hear all about it. Ruining someone's life is right up their alley.

Barti orders herself a chai latte, as she doesn't drink coffee. Caffeine gives her nasty stomach pains. While she waits for her drink to be made she notices the front cover of the newspaper on one of the unoccupied tables. Dirty dishes yet to be cleaned from that same table. The paper is left open by the previous reader on page 12. The headline reads '35-Year Anniversary of Brutal Asylum Slayings'.

Barti reads on to find out it's about the infamous multiple murders at Larundel Asylum committed by Edgar Sanchez.

Barti fell victim to psychological trauma and bullying back in her school days; days she tries to forget. She was pushed and made to be an outcast by the group of people she now calls friends.

At a school disco Barti had danced with multiple boys, and Suzi had decided to spread a rumour. Not one, but multiple. She told everyone Barti had kissed all the boys she had danced with, was fingered by Zac, and fucked Mike. The entire school had found out and they began calling her things that no one would want to hear. Far from the truth of her normal life. Barti was devastated.

Suzi had come to school early Monday morning and noticed Barti sitting on the bench crying. She wanted to ask her what the matter was but there was no point. She already knew why.

Over the years, Barti has moved on and has successfully made a career out of bullies. She is a junior paralegal, working for a large firm in Melbourne called Buchanan Law. Years of hard work and endless late nights of studying has paid off. She has recently forgiven the girls for their outlandish and childish treatment of her back in the school days, and for giving her mental health issues. She has learnt to live with LTS (Lifetime Trauma Syndrome), but she can never forget what they're capable of. She's seen it firsthand. The scars remain, but the heart ponders. Accepting the past is the only thing she could have done to move forward.

After the café, they enter the invitation shop. It is pristine and elegant. Hundreds upon hundreds of designs for all occasions to choose from. The girls spend hours trying to decide on the right one. They end up going with an original design that Suzi made herself, of course.

The moment Suzi opens the invite, her phone is in hand and a call is placed straight to Betty, who is her Maid of Honour. They both giggle like little school girls. Betty also received her invite, and they chat about how wonderful the invitations look and how great the big day is going to be.

Betty is curious about the second little envelope inside, but doesn't mention anything to Suzi. Betty doesn't remember them ever talking about it or ordering them at all. Suzi must have gone back by herself on a separate day to plan it – one of those rare occasions Suzi had done something without Betty.

Curiosity gets the better of Betty. She wants to … no, she *needs* to know what is inside the smaller enveloper. But on the front, there is writing:

Please open on wedding night
when bridal party is all alone.
Sealed Surprise

The immediate bridal party is booked to stay two nights in the Arlberg Hotham Lodge, a six-bedroom hotel that sits on top of Mount Hotham in the Alpine Ranges.

Suzi and Anthony have booked the entire lodge for the group, strictly no parents. Not that she's embarrassed of her mum and dad – they are paying for it, so you would think they had some say. But guess again: the newlyweds would rather kick it with their mates and enjoy the first night as Mr. & Mrs. McCollough than have oldies there to watch their every move.

Betty doesn't wait any longer. She has held her tongue long enough. Her heart beating fast, fear of asking holds her back for a few seconds longer before she asks, 'What's in the sealed envelope?'

'Exactly what it says – a sealed surprise.'

'I think the Maid of Honour should know. Don't you?'

'I think it should remain a secret.'

They both giggle. Then Suzi admits she doesn't know either. Half the surprise.

'Really? Aren't you curious?'

'Yes, I'm fuckin' curious, but it's my wedding and I say we leave it a secret. It must be a surprise from the invitation place. They're so thoughtful. I'll be really pissed if anyone opens it and spoils the surprise. You better let them know not to open it. Got it, B?'

'Sure, no problem. I'll let everyone know not to open it. This is so exciting, Suz. It's going to be the best day ever.'

'I know, right?'

If Suzi didn't blow her own trumpet, then Betty is right there to do it for her. Like two peas seeded from the same pod.

The plan is set in motion.

Taken hook, line and sinker.

Chapter 3

27 February 2022

I couldn't believe my fucking eyes. Suzi Dawson came into the shop today. I froze in my boots. If I hadn't gone earlier, I would have shat myself, literally.

I prayed to God that she wouldn't recognise me.

Well, she didn't.

I've changed a lot since school. I look way different now. Maybe some features remain the same but from that alone she wouldn't know who I was. Even my name has changed.

I'm trying to delete everything from those days. Nothing good came from it.

I lie. Hatred for Suzi is what came from it. That's a good thing.

I walked away from school, ashamed and embarrassed. Fucking Suzi Dawson and her mob of bitches. I had always hoped they'd die a painful death. I should have just killed her there and then in the store when I had the chance. But then again, I wouldn't get away with it and I would spend the rest of my life in jail. I would have been caught like a fish in a net.

She had that bitch Betty with her and some other girl. It looked like Elizabeth Sinclair, but I couldn't be sure. She was nice, so much like me. Not physically, but … victim-ly. I know that's not a word but I'm using it anyway. No one can run my life anymore.

She didn't say much. She just smiled and agreed with what they said. She dressed smart, like she has a fancy career. I didn't want to ask and blow my cover. Like myself, she had been bullied by them. They treated so many of us like shit. They ruined my life, especially that Anthony. He'll get his and when he does, I want to be there to see it.

I want to say I can't believe that Suzi and Anthony are getting married, but it was written back then. Everyone knew they would. Plus, they're made for each other. They suit each other like flies to shit.

I can't believe that out of all the printing shops in Melbourne, they happen to come to this one. I mean, what are the fuckin' chances, seriously? One in a billion. Only my guestimate.

She ordered 176 invites. I wonder how many will agree to attend. I bet there would be heaps who will be too afraid to decline.

No, stop thinking like that.

That is maniacally mean, but I love it.

No, you don't.

Think about it before you say no.

I have.

No, you haven't.

This is what's going on in my head. My evil thoughts and my good thoughts, always trying to outdo one another. I love them both dearly.

Maybe I can play a joke. Just a little one. I won't follow through with it. I just want to scare her. Wouldn't it be great to see her reaction? Yes, it would.

I will make the best invites I have ever made. Suzi gave me the design she wants. She'll get that with a tad more love put into them. This plan I've just thought of will be great. But only if they follow the instructions on the little envelope.

If they don't, well, then I have a Plan B. Plan C can wait, for now. First things first: send Elizabeth a friend request on Facebook. If she accepts, then Suzi will request me as friend – she won't let Elizabeth have me as a friend and not her.

I don't want to say I told you so, but I will: I told you so. Elizabeth accepted my friend request in no time. Wow, so fast. Then within minutes I had a new friend request – Suzi Dawson wants to be my friend. That schmuck look on her face in the profile pic. Fuck, I hate her.

Well, I'm happy to say my plan has begun and it's going to be a cracker. Wouldn't it be funny if I got invited to the wedding? Now that would be hilarious.

Suzi and Betty might be the evil twins, but I know a thing about evil. Evil killer. Stop it lol lol lol.

Let the planning begin.

Chapter 4

The wedding is approaching fast and still so much needs to be done. March is around the corner and the fabric has just arrived from Milan.

The first fitting of the dresses has commenced, and the trio of Italian dressmakers have to work overtime to get them ready for Suzi. What Suzi wants, Suzi gets.

Her brother Craig is going out with an Italian girl named Karina. Karina's mum, Anna, Aunt Selina, and Nonna Rosa own a dressmaking business. They design and alter clothing for every occasion, but specialise in weddings. Rosa started this business back when she first came to Australia in the 60s. Rosa and her husband, Pasquale, migrated Down Under from Milan for a better life – the best move they ever made. Life has unfolded just as they had planned.

Craig was asked – actually ordered – not to be there today. Suzi didn't want anyone from the bridal party besides the girls to see her in her dress, or the girls in theirs. Karina was also told she wasn't allowed in there, banished from her own house. The closest Karina got was seeing the girls walk in.

Suzi doesn't think much of Karina. She thinks Karina has a big mouth and will gossip about the dresses. Karina has her own thoughts about Suzi, which she keeps to herself. But Karina's annoyance with Suzi deepens when she learns she has matched Craig with someone else for the bridal party couples, a friend from school.

Craig will spend the entire day and evening with some bimbo Karina doesn't know. She will be forced to sit with her mum and dad on a table that will most likely be right at the back, looking at the back of people's heads. Suzi would have done this on purpose so Karina doesn't interfere with Craig. His sole focus for the evening should be on his sister, his only job for the day. That's the kind of bitch Suzi is.

If it wasn't for the job and money, Karina's mum would have declined the work and told her where to go. But 'a job is a job', Nonna Rosa has always said. The boys have their fittings the following week. Today, Craig will spend the day with Anthony and the boys. They have planned a trip up to Yarra Glen. The wineries will be submerged with immature testosterone – career-driven, spoilt kids with unsociable attitudes, deeper than their pockets.

Anthony volunteers his friend George to drive. Luckily for them, George doesn't care because he doesn't drink. It's the aftermath he's worried about. With drinking too much comes being sick and that dreadful vomit stage. He's not looking forward to that.

The dresses hang on the racks, resembling Frankenstein – pieces of fabric and material botched together. The colour Suzi has chosen for her dress is pretty – a pastel off-white. It is cut just above the knee, a length Suzi is adamant they get right. The bridesmaids' dresses go all the way down to their ankles.

Suzi's eyes light up like a kid in a candy store when she lays eyes on them. She is so impressed, her smile almost rips the commissure – the skin that attaches the top and bottom lip.

'B-b-bellissima,' is all she can muster. It's probably the only Italian word she knows that's not rude, provocative, or offensive.

'Oh, my goodness. They look gorgeous,' says Barti.

'Did you expect anything less from me? I mean, just take a look? My wedding will be a photographer's dream, don't you think?'

Barti feels belittled by Suzi's comment. She really knows how to put someone down. Barti sometimes feels like Suzi hasn't really changed since her school days. Barti would love to have the strength to drop everything and walk out. Tell Suzi how she really feels and be done with this monster. Barti wants to walk out right that minute and never look back – if she only had the courage.

But she is better than that. She has learned to channel her feelings and anger, filter the bad, caress the good. She doesn't spend that much time with Suzi to warrant an outbreak, even though she comes across like the plague sometimes. A part of Barti feels sorry for her. Easy to understand if you knew her parents. The wrong lessons were taught to her, hence the wrong attitude towards others.

The other friend with them today is Julie. Fiery and opinionated when she knows she is right, humble and pleasant when she gets it wrong. Always out to have a great time. Sometimes, she is so quiet you forget she's in the room. Not today though; something is bothering her.

At school her brother had been picked on and bullied by Anthony and his goons. She tried to stick up for him many times but was cut down by Suzi. It was always a do or die situation with Suzi. If you did, then you would die. Julie wasn't allowed to defend her own brother. She was given an ultimatum, us or him. She loved the 'us' part too much and forgot about him. His heart was broken and there was no mending or coming back from that.

'OMG, Suzi, you are just so gorgeous,' says Betty, followed by a wolf whistle. 'Look at you in that dress!'

'I know, B. My figure is perfect for this dress. This is simply the best design, I'm so glad I found it. This won't suit anyone else but me. Don't you think?'

She looks over to the girls for approval. They wouldn't dare say anything negative. They know better and also know they would be straight out of the bridal party with their tails tucked between their legs if they say anything Suzi doesn't like. That's the type of person this bridezilla is. Even her parents fear her.

Betty speaks first, seeing she is the 2IC. She leads the pack when Suzi isn't there, which isn't that often.

'You look gorge, babe. I mean, look at you. Seriously. Anthony's so lucky to have you.'

Then a voice from the back changes the mood and pierces the air like someone put a pin to a balloon.

'Don't you think the dress is too short, Suz?'

They turn in horror. Flames fire out from Suzi's eyes, targeted towards Julie. The raging bull is about to charge the matador's muleta. Betty's mouth mimes the words that Julie can make out.

You're dead, bitch.

'What did you say?' asks Suzi.

You could hear the sound of a pin drop. Everything went dead silent.

'I said … I said, isn't the dress a little short?'

Suzi turns to face the mirror, ignoring Julie and admiring her reflection in the mirror. Queen Nefertiti at her best. She has zoned out from what has just been said and has zoned into her own beauty. Only she can see what she sees.

Voices are muffled around her. White noise. The only sound she hears is that little voice in her head telling her how beautiful she is. She is reminded constantly by friends and family that she is Cinderella with all her beauty. The beauty without her beast, Snow White with magical pretty looks.

This Snow White has her prince, and together they will rule the roost. But there is more than just a witch who would love to see her downfall, her soul crushed. She is a marked woman.

'I will pretend you didn't say that, Julie,' she says, drawing out her name. 'That foul shit that dribbled out of your mouth. I don't want you to say another word for the rest of the fitting. Not a FUCKING WORD.'

And that's how the rest of the fittings continue. They all know who the boss is, and would never dare to cross her.

The dresses are pinned, the hems rolled up and the length measured to perfection. All is set for one more fitting that should be the last before the big day.

Suzi gives the dressmakers a new deadline. She wants them two weeks earlier than originally planned.

'But Miss Dawson, this will put a lot of pressure on us. We still have so much work to be done. Your ask is almost impossible. We have other clients, other dresses to be finished before yours. Their weddings are weeks before yours,' said Anna with a worried look.

'So, what you're saying is that you can't do it? Or you won't do it?'

'I'm not saying that at all. I'm just saying we will struggle to get it done four weeks before your wedding. I don't want to rush it.'

Suzi looks at them as if they have done her an injustice. Like they had murdered her dream.

'Do I need to look elsewhere to get these done, Anna? I mean, I can easily find someone else who will be more than happy to help me with this crisis I am experiencing.'

Anna speaks briefly to Nonna Rosa. The two exchange words in Italian. Julie lets out a soft muted giggle when she hears Rosa throw out the word 'putana' a few times. It was said in a low tone that Suzi didn't hear what Nonna Rosa had called her. Julie and her brother have called Suzi that exact word many times before. 'Slut' is a word that is regularly used describing Suzi. The thought of him brings a tear to her eyes. She wipes it discreetly.

'Okay, Mama Rosa said it *can* be done. We will have a fitting four weeks before the wedding.'

The calendar is marked with the time and date. 29th May at 1:00 in the afternoon. Both parties agree and leave it at that.

The tension in the room is so thick you could cut it with a knife. A knife that could find its way into this story.

Chapter 5

(Police Interview: Elizabeth Sinclair – 27th June 2023)

Detective Louie Taylor: Hi Elizabeth. Can I get you anything?

Elizabeth: No. No, I'm fine thank you.

Detective Louie Taylor: I want to introduce myself. My name's Detective Louie Taylor and this is my partner Detective Donna Zammit. We're from the Albury Criminal Investigation Department. We have a few questions to ask you that could help us with the investigation. Do you know why you're here?

Elizabeth: Yes, I do. The murder.

Detective Louie Taylor: Yes, the murder. What can you tell us about it?

Elizabeth: Where do I begin?

Detective Donna Zammit: From the start please, Elizabeth. What do you remember about the day?

Elizabeth: We were up early. Suzi had us up at 5:00am. The hairdresser was there at 5:15. I remember that because I always set up a second alarm after the first, fifteen minutes after.

Detective Louie Taylor: Do you always do that with the alarm or was it just for the wedding? I just find it a little strange that someone would do that.

Elizabeth: What's so strange about setting up more than one alarm? A lot of people do it.

Detective Louie Taylor: I don't. I stick with one alarm and then I'm out of bed.

Elizabeth: Well good for you, detective. The last time I checked, setting up more than one alarm wasn't a criminal offence.

Detective Donna Zammit: I set more than one, Lou. My sister got me onto it when we were younger. What happened after the arrival of the hairdresser?

Elizabeth: Suzi got her hair done first. She said it was going to take the longest. She had to have the first shower too.

Detective Louie Taylor: Were you or any of the girls angry about that?

Elizabeth: No, detective, I was okay with it and so were the others.

Detective Louie Taylor: So, no words were exchanged? Tempers didn't flare?

Elizabeth: No. No one got angry. Only ...

Detective Louie Taylor: Only what? Did something happen?

Elizabeth: Well ... kinda. Nothing serious, just. Okay. Suzi has a bad habit of pissing people off. She can get under your skin, if you know what I mean.

Detective Louie Taylor: Okay. Go on.

Elizabeth: She said something that got us ... annoyed.

Detective Donna Zammit: What did she say?

Elizabeth: She said that she had a secret about each of us and if any one of us tried to ruin her wedding day, that she was going to tell the world what they were. She was going to post shit on Snapchat and Facebook.

Detective Donna Zammit: And did she know things about you all that you want kept quiet?

Elizabeth: Something like that. I bet you would feel the same way, Detective Zammit.

Detective Donna Zammit: Maybe. We all have them, those little secrets. The thing is, secrets aren't meant to be shared with anyone. They belong to you. Isn't that right, Elizabeth?

Elizabeth: You asked me what happened, so I told you.

Detective Louie Taylor: So, which one of you did it?

Chapter 6

The final fittings and dress rehearsals went better than expected. The group was all satisfied with the final product. The dress was slick and fit like a snug glove.

Everyone seemed happy. Surprisingly, so too did Suzi. She did seem a little reserved for some reason. Something on her mind? Probably the pressure of the wedding. It can take a lot out of you mentally – stress the obvious outcome.

The Hen's Night and Buck's Party are scheduled on the same night. They have booked different venues. The girls are going to the Chaise Lounge on Queen Street, a venue they're all too familiar with. They've spent endless Saturday nights dancing, drinking, partying, and everything else that comes with it.

The boys, on the other hand, are off to The Spice Market where a boozy evening could turn ugly if they're not careful. It only takes one dickhead to create a scene. A few months back Marlon started chatting to a few girls. It began innocently but turned ugly the minute he grabbed one of the girl's boob. He got a handful before the girl's boyfriend got a fistful into him. Things turned from bad to worse when a knife was produced. Marlon didn't see it come his way and had his arm slashed. Bouncers pounced on the other guy, and he was held in the storeroom until police arrived. Luckily for Marlon it was only a flesh wound.

Pre-party drinks are held at Betty's, who lives alone. Less than six months ago she was living with her boyfriend, Tim, who turned out to be a Grade A jerk. A dead-set dropkick. Unemployed and useless, a shell of a man. He spent the entire day sleeping and playing PlayStation. The arguments got out of hand. Some days so did he. Violence was the only way he knew how to solve a problem. Several black eyes later, Anthony and his mates had had enough and paid him an unscheduled visit to smooth things out.

By the time Betty had arrived back home one evening, Tim had left an apology letter and a huge wad of cash for rent and damages. He was nowhere to be seen, or heard from. She never meant any harm to him, but there was no harm in returning the favour. The last she'd heard he had moved back to Ballarat and moved in with a mate, with benefits. It stopped there. She didn't want to know any more about the visit the boys had paid him. The less she knew the better.

The flat is packed with girls. Music blaring from the smart speaker, a Spotify playlist carefully selected by the host, Taylor Swift shaking it up. Drinks and nibbles aplenty. More alcohol than food. The girls had been monitoring their food intake. Suzi has them all on a strict eating regime. No fast food for the month before the wedding. They need to snuggle into their dresses. No limit on alcohol, though. Tonight is proving that theory.

A variety of drinks are placed on the table. Vodka, gin, Baileys. Cranberry juice and tonic to complement the first two drinks, and beer and cider for the girls who don't want something sweet. Barti loves beer, and pale ale is her favourite. She's never the fussy one to stick to one type, though – whatever is on offer will do.

Suzi started drinking once they'd left the rehearsals. They stopped at a drive-through bottle shop and bought the alcohol. They also picked up a travel pack for the rest of the drive home. Suzi was the only one drinking in the car – her party, her rules. No one had a say.

Suzi starts to get louder than usual, louder than the music. The girls are all chatting about their school days. They had brought back some saucy memories, and some not so. Most of the girls there had gone to the same private school. Only a handful hadn't. Haileybury private school in Brighton saw the worst this mob could administer; Team Anthony taking it to another level for the boys.

The bullying started when both groups were formed, back in Year Eight. From that day forth, the school grounds where deemed 'The Danger Zone'. The injury list was so extensive, an ambulance visit once a week was common. Some weeks twice.

There was one boy they remembered being a victim, bullied by both groups relentlessly. No one could remember his name. They probably didn't take time to find that out. They do remember him being gay and having a thing for Anthony. Cruelty is such a bitch, especially when it's done to you. This kid copped heaps from them. It lasted a long time until one day he stopped coming to classes. He never attended sport; actually, he never attended school in general. They all felt sorry for him, except Suzi. She just kept on laughing and laughing, story after story. *Poor gay guy,* they thought.

They were surprised he never retaliated or planned for revenge. No one knew what had happened to him after that, so life went back to normal for the group. They eventually found other victims. One door closes, five others open.

Julie knew exactly who they were talking about. It was her brother. She played dumb and kept to herself, not joining in the conversation.

Ubers dropped them all off at different times in front of the venue. Girls at one, the boys at the other. The queue of people waiting to get in is long. If the patrons combined, they could have easily contributed to a thirty-metre Chinese dragon. One guess who would be at the head? The ass end would fit her better.

The Uber that had Julie, Barti, and a few of the other girls ended up being the last to arrive. A greasy look is thrown their way by Suzi. A look that says, 'What fuckin' kept you?'

'The driver stopped for petrol,' Julie explains, the only one game enough to speak. The matter on hand is abruptly halted with a palm up to Julie's face.

The weather isn't pleasant to be waiting in queues. Drops of rain had begun the moment they stepped out of the cars. The last thing they want is to wait in the queue and get rained on. Wet hair plus runny make-up equals drowned cat lookalike.

Luckily Suzi knows the head bouncer out the front of the venue. He lets them in as members. It pays to know people in the right areas. Word has it she once gave him a blowjob in the toilets when she and Anthony were on a break. She seems to get her way, all the time.

The music is pumping, drinks passed around like pollen from person to person. A booth had been booked for the group. Fourteen girls in total. Fourteen different attitudes, but only one who is in charge.

A complimentary bottle of champagne is delivered by a very hot busboy. Carl introduces himself as their personal waiter for the evening. Swedish-born, blonde with chiselled features, three-day stubble and a chest that looked like it is carved out of stone. His tight shirt clings onto his sweaty skin like it is another layer. Their night just got even better.

'Anything you want, just ask,' says Carl in his hot Swedish accent.

'Anything?' asks Suzi with a smile, eyes moving down to his dick. Her thoughts are written all over her face. No secret there. They both exchange a smile before Carl leaves with the first order. The sash draped across the chest of Suzi lets everyone know she is a bride to be ... but isn't one *yet*. What happens in Vegas, stays in Vegas, isn't that what they say?

The drinks come furiously fast. One after the other, the count going out the window. The air is moist, the atmosphere wild, and the girls are a few drinks away from being drunk. Carl must have walked 30,000 steps within the first hour. He is really good with remembering drink orders and hasn't stuffed up once. One round of drinks ended up being lit up on fire. Double the dosage of the alcoholic volume. A quick and easy way to end your night prematurely.

Suzi stands up and almost topples over. She has to hold on to the couch to stabilise herself. The whole room spins like a merry-go-round, but she is the only one on it. She looks around for support. The others are all laughing and checking out the guys, grabbing a few of them on the butt as they walk by. Suzi is looking around to see where the female toilets are. She can feel a barf coming on and needs to move quickly before it projectiles out like in *The Exorcist*. She could never cope with the embarrassment.

She tries to muster up the strength to say something to the girls but they are too loud and not paying any attention to her. It's hard to hear anything in this place, even if you yell in one's ear. A whisper amongst the loud music falls on deaf ears, her voice lost between the beats. Suzi turns and makes her way out of the booth towards the toilet, passing the bar. Carl puts his hand out to stop her. He says something that she can't understand. Either that or she doesn't hear him. She says yes to whatever he said and keeps walking to the toilet.

She pushes the door open and walks into a dim, dingy toilet block. The music still loud in her ears, the bathroom her only solace from the doof-doofing coming from the other side of the wall. Her ears slowly adjust. Her vision is still not the best; something alcohol is renowned for.

A couple of girls standing in front of the mirror complain about a boyfriend. 'Dump him,' says one of them, and they giggle.

Suzi locks herself in the cubicle. Pulls the seat down, lifts her dress up and undies down, and sits there, trying to get her thoughts together. She is already beginning to forget half the night. She hears the door open and close. The noise has mellowed, which gives her the indication the two girls left. She is finally alone.

After dry retching a few times, she pulls her undies up and dress back down, feeling behind her in case any toilet paper stuck to her arse. No vomit surfaced on this visit. Maybe the next one.

Once she is satisfied with her dress code and sees she doesn't have any unwanted accessories dangling behind her, she unlocks the door and walks out from the cubicle. She notices someone by the tap. She hadn't heard the door reopen. She assumed she was alone. She walks over and stands next to them, turns on the tap, and begins to wash her hands. She looks over at this other person in the mirror.

'I know you, don't I?' says Suzi, slurring her words.

The woman looks at Suzi through the mirror before turning around and walking out. Suzi turns and follows her with her eyes. She notices a smile on the woman's face. It is the last thought she remembers before she collapses and passes out.

On the other side of town, the boys have their own little thing going on. Dirty thoughts at the forefront of their minds. Craig was not invited, reason being that he's Suzi's brother. The less he knows, the less she will find out. Anthony doesn't want her knowing anything that might go on tonight.

George is starting to get annoyed by always being the designated driver. 'George do this, George do that.' He's fucking sick of it. That's what he told Craig via text. He trusts Craig won't say anything. He trusts him more than any of the others – they have a special bond that only they can understand.

The Spice Market is just as busy as the Chaise Lounge. Girls overpopulate the boys 3:1. That's just the way Anthony prefers it. He has his close mates with him, the ones who will take a bullet for him or even the wrap for a heinous crime. If it came down to it, these boys wouldn't say a word.

Four make up the team of Anthony's posse. Outlaws in their own minds, superheroes to the opposite sex. Anthony stands out as the tough guy, the handsome Han Solo of the group. He has them eating out of his palm. The couple-to-be have so many similar traits. If you asked Dexter from the show *A Perfect Match*, he would give them a compatibility score of 100%.

George was asked to go and buy the first round of drinks. The boys wanted to hang back and check out the girls on the podium. Short skirts matching the boys' short IQs. The first round of drinks arrive. George places four bourbon and Cokes on the table. High fives are thrown around that Borat would be proud of. The night goes as planned with drink after drink. Down the hatch, making its way down the bottomless pit. These boys can really drink.

At some point in the evening, George makes a break. He is fed up with hanging about like a bad smell. He clearly isn't having a good time, so he decides to lash on the guys. George leaves without saying a word to the others. Anthony and the others are none the wiser. They don't even notice him going. Just goes to show what they really think of him.

Marlon tells Anthony that there's a girl looking over this way. He puts his glass down and makes that short trip down to the other table. She's there with two other girls. They acknowledge his arrival and stand up. They whisper something in their friend's ear and then leave her all alone with Anthony. He makes short work of this meeting. Within a few minutes they are up and heading to the dancefloor. Anthony's friends cheer him on, yelling compliments that later could be a mistake. Something these boys never seem to get right.

Anthony and the girl bypass the dancefloor and head straight out the door. Anthony doesn't return. He vanishes in the night like a vampire.

Chapter 7

29 May 2023

The inside trading worked wonders. I found out where Suzi and her clan were going to be. From the photos of them on Facebook, angled in such a way that nobody would see the dresses, the fitting proved to be a success. Smiles all around. But I've seen them, and they are the ugliest dresses I've ever seen. If Suzi was in front of me now, I would tell her that to her face.

How do I know what the dresses look like? A mystery to be revealed soon.

I would have also introduced her to some pain. I wouldn't bother hurting my fist by punching her. Maybe I should just drive a knife into her back, like she has done to so many others, including me. The bitch deserves everything she gets, and everything she is going to get.

I followed her and her fake friends to a club. OMG, there are so many reasons why I don't go clubbing. Full of losers and try-hards. I felt like an undercover agent, stealth mode. I disguised myself really well. She wouldn't have worked out it was me. It's amazing what a little make-up can do.

She looked so schmuck with her friends. She was probably too drunk to even notice me there, watching her from a distance. I saw the way she eyed off that guy bringing the drinks. I bet she wanted to fuck him.

Dirty whore.

She's wearing that sash like she wants the world to know she's getting married but at the back of her mind she has the thought of the busboy lingering, thinking of him naked. Busboy didn't see me slip the pills in her drink. None of her friends did either.

She almost made me when she saw me in the toilet. She asked me where she knew me from. I wasn't too worried, as she wouldn't remember a thing the following day. You gotta love roofies. She went down like a sack of shit. It would have been so easy to smother her while she lay there unconscious. But that place was crawling with bouncers and cameras. They would have seen me go into the restrooms, and my plan would have fallen through before the end of the night. The day and time to get her is just around the corner. She is no better than her cheating man, that sly prick.

I left after Suzi went down for the three count. I knew where Anthony and his friends were going to be. The best thing ever invented is cameras on phones. I rang a couple of friends and asked if they wanted to go out for a drink. Fucking Anthony that night in his car was payback. Poor Suzi. She's going to be surprised and pissed when these photos pop up, at the right time, of course. Tick tock, tick tock – time is almost up.

P.S. He wasn't that good. I bet she isn't either.

Chapter 8

(Police Interview: Craig Dawson – 27 June 2023)

Detective Louie Taylor: Hi Craig, you know who we are, we introduced ourselves a little while ago. How are you feeling? Can we get you anything?

Craig shakes his head.

Detective Louie Taylor: Okay. Tell us about the threat your sister made to the other girls. Did that also apply to the boys?

Craig: I'm not sure.

Detective Louie Taylor: You're not sure about what, Craig? Please be clear with your answers. We don't want to be here all night going round in circles.

Craig: I'm not sure if it applied to the guys. I doubt it would. The guys wanted to see this through.

Detective Donna Zammit: So, what you're saying is that the girls didn't want to see Suzi marry Anthony? Was there anything going on that you can tell us?

Craig: How would I know? I was always left out of things.

Detective Donna Zammit: Did your sister say anything to you about anyone wanting to hurt her?

Detective Louie Taylor: Look mate, I can see you're tearing up. I know it's hard, but we want to get to the bottom of this. If there is anything you know, anything you can tell us that might help with this investigation, please do so now.

Detective Donna Zammit: My partner is right. We want to get to the bottom of this before anyone else gets hurt. Did your sister say anything to you that you found odd?

Craig: She was scared of something leading up to the wedding. That day of the dress rehearsals, she came home with a worried look on her face. When I asked her what was wrong, she said something about stalkers on Facebook. I think she was harassed on social media. That's all I know.

Detective Donna Zammit: Okay, that's great. That's very helpful.

Craig: Also, that night of her hen's night, she said her drink was spiked. She also said she thinks she recognised someone in the toilet. Maybe they did something to her drink. Surely the club would have cameras in there. Check them. You might see something useful.

Detective Louie Taylor: That's what we wanted to know. Thanks Craig, you've been an awesome help.

Chapter 9

TWO DEAD, ONE INJURED IN

MELBOURNE WEDDING TRAGEDY

Report by Sarah Patterson – 26 June 2023

Two people are dead and one seriously injured when a bridal party honeymoon sleepover turned deadly. The two victims, who cannot be identified at this time, were believed to have been from the same family. The injured woman was airlifted to the Royal Melbourne Hospital where she is in a serious but stable condition.

The ceremony of Anthony McCollough, 28, and Suzi Dawson, 27, was held at Bright Centenary Park. A spokesperson for the couple said both had been waiting for this day since secondary college.

Celebrant Victoria Larsen said the ceremony went as planned.

'The couple and guests were so well behaved. Tears were shed as one would expect at a wedding.'

She also said she had not noticed anything out of the ordinary. Family and friends of the victims were shocked to hear what had happened.

Flowers have been laid out the front of the lodge by mourners. An ongoing investigation is underway. More news to follow as it comes through.

Chapter 10

That special day in June that Suzi had been waiting for has arrived. The weather is perfect, like it had been purchased online and dumped over Bright. Life expectancy of twenty-four hours.

The quartet is playing soft angelic music in the background, while the guests make their way to their seats, program in hand like they are about to witness the premiere of *Mamma Mia! The Musical.*

The birds have a front row seat, nestled comfortably in the trees with the best aerial view of the wedding; human lovebirds are on centre stage. The air has excitement flowing through it, with a slight breeze bringing serenity to the mood. The flow of the river separates the music from nature, together making a sound so heavenly you would think you've died and gone directly to Led Zeppelin's stairway to heaven.

Not all the guests invited had replied with their RSVP. Some didn't take the time to return a message that they weren't attending. A pet hate any couple organising a wedding would agree with. From the original number of invites only twenty had not responded, so there is a fair number of butts seated on seats.

The groom and his groomsmen are in position, standing up the front with Victoria Larsen, the celebrant, waiting for the main quartet piece to be played, indicating that the main attraction has turned up.

Nerves had arrived before the bride. A pool of sweat forms under Anthony's hairline. His mates are trying their best to keep him calm, but they're boys; they don't know anything about keeping calm. 'Skol a beer,' would be their only advice. Alcohol solves all problems to them.

The music lowers to a hum, almost unnoticeable. It remains that way for about half a minute. The longest thirty seconds Anthony has ever felt. He knows it's time. SHE, has arrived. His bride, his future wife, his main attraction is here.

The quartet begin to play *Ave Maria*, filling the spaces between people. The gardens are lit up with sounds and lyrics, stunning effects like being at a Celine Dion concert, with only her saintly voice echoing from the speakers. The bride is present and she wants the world to know it.

The bridesmaids make their traditional march down the aisle. Betty lays the path with her footprints, setting the scene for the star. Barti and Julie make up the chain gang in sync. Girls and guys are finally in position, exchanging looks with a smile. Eyes in the audience adjust to the performance laid before them.

Heads turn simultaneously towards the back to view a tall, beautiful woman, arm wrapped around an elegant distinguished gentleman, her father, for the final voyage as a single woman. The dress is perfect, matching the weather, her hair stunning, every strand in place, her shoes more expensive than the boys' suits put together.

Ed Sheeran's *Perfect* begins to play once *Ave Maria* fades out, completing the perfect entrance. All eyes are on Suzi. The perfect bride, the perfect wife, the perfect friend. These thoughts are only in her head, fabricated amongst many other thoughts that only her head contains. She is blind to every other thought about her. A narcissist.

Tears begin to flow from some of the guests, as this wonderful moment is coming to life right before their eyes. The stage is all hers and she is working this runway to perfection. She embraces this opportunity and savours the moment like it's her last.

There is a smile under her veil that doesn't seem real; a look that indicates she is hiding something deep down inside her, something she won't let surface and ruin the moment. She seems happy but the happiness looks fake. What could possibly be on her mind. Nerves? She's been distracted in the weeks leading up to this day. Something has happened that she hasn't mentioned to anyone. Whatever it is, it has been locked away in the vault for another time.

The song is still playing while she reaches the end of the line. Her father turns to her and gives her a kiss on her cheek, his lips meeting the rough material of the veil. Anthony makes his way towards them and shakes hands with Ashton, Suzi's dad. He takes position next to her. He lifts her veil and plants one of many more kisses to come on her lips. A slight hesitation from Suzi makes Anthony hesitate, his smile brought down to half-mast.

Her smile reassures him things are still okay. The words, 'Let's proceed,' from the celebrant gets everyone in position. Their hands drop in front of them to wait for Victoria to begin. The moment of truth, or death is here.

'Good afternoon, my name is Victoria Jensen and I am the celebrant for today's ceremony. I am authorised to solemnise marriages according to the law in Australia. I declare that this marriage is truthful and legitimate and will stand as a legal marriage.

We are gathered here today in the face of this company, to join together Anthony McCollough and Suzi Dawson in matrimony; which is an honourable and solemn estate and therefore is not to be entered into unadvisedly or soberly, who will be making a pledge to each other to be true, faithful, loving and devoted to one another.'

Anthony can feel the tension between them rise after the words, 'true, faithful, loving and devoted.'

Has he been all of those to Suzi? Of course, he has … not. There is no doubt he loves her. He is always true to her, but that word 'faithful' lingers in his thought for a while. That is one word he needs to work on if this marriage is going to work, or more so, last. He knows there were slip-ups from time to time. He has convinced himself that's all they were.

Suzi and he have been together for a very long time. Surely every couple has slip-ups? Don't they?

Has Suzi slipped up? Anthony panics at that thought. His beautiful and faithful fiancé, soon to be his wife, might not have been faithful. This thought brings doubt to his feelings. Do they really love each other or is this a complete and utter mistake? Is it too late to pull out now? He knows there is some part of the ceremony where they give someone a chance to speak up, object to the marriage going ahead. What if he speaks up? Has that ever been done before? The groom speaking up for himself? What would be the reaction from the guests, friends, and family? What would be the reaction from Suzi?

The celebrant has stopped talking. All eyes are on Anthony. *What has just happened? Has someone said something and they're waiting on me to respond? They must have. It's my wedding.* Suzi is looking at him, waiting for him to speak.

'Sorry, could you repeat what you just said? I didn't hear you.' He looks over to Suzi with apologetic eyes.

'Sure. Do you, Anthony, take Suzi for your lawful wedded wife, to be joined in matrimony? Will you love, honour, comfort, and cherish her from this day forward, forsaking all others, keeping only unto her for as long as you both shall live?'

The air is filled with stillness, like God has muted the world until Anthony answers the question. A question that makes time freeze. All these words are thrown his way and he doesn't have an answer for them.

For as long as you both shall live.

More like until she kills me.

He thinks fast, the only words that he can and should muster escape his lips. His breath is withdrawn and is captured with fear midway down.

'I do.'

The celebrant repeats everything she said to Anthony, this time to Suzi. There's no hesitation in her answer. The ceremony is now flowing the way it should. A smile reappears on Suzi's face, one that Anthony is all too familiar with. One he is comfortable with. One he fell in love with. Now for the words that will seal this marriage.

'I now pronounce that you are husband and wife. You may now seal this marriage with a kiss.'

They finally kiss.

'Ladies and gentleman, I present to you the new couple, Mr. and Mrs. Anthony McCollough.'

Loud cheers from the guests startle the birds in the trees. They fly off to find another group to be entertained by. Hugs and kisses from both the groomsmen and bridesmaids, parents and friends. Photos will be taken at the park, parents the only people to stay on for them. The rest will meet at the reception venue for drinks and finger food.

That look in Suzi's eyes is back, but it's not only directed towards Anthony. She has a new victim in view.

One of her bridesmaids.

Chapter 11

I sat at the back so no one recognised me. I had my hair up and a dark lipstick to match my tight, off the shoulder dress. I sat amongst a group of old farts. They bored me silly with their talk about lawn bowls. I hate lawn bowls and I don't ever want to grow old for that reason. I hope I don't turn out like them.

I watched Anthony from a distance, knowing something Suzi doesn't. OMG, I slept with the groom last month lol. Serves you right, you bitch. I finally got what I was meant to get back in high school. I know Anthony wanted me. But that bitch ruined everything and he lied to get himself out of it.

A bug flew into my eye during the ceremony and I had a tear because of it. The old bag next to me, Yvonne I think her name was, passed over a snot rag. Are you seriously giving me a hanky that you've used? What I said and what I wanted to say were two different things. I didn't want to cause a scene and get noticed.

The music by far was the best part of the day. Suzi arrived in a horse-drawn carriage. She should have been the one pulling the carriage. Her dad has always been by her side, no matter what. I almost vomited when I saw her dress. It was terrible. So glad she was wearing it and not me.

I always wondered if I had ended up with Anthony, would she have come to our wedding? What would she have thought of my dress? Well, I'm wearing a black dress because I can also use it for her funeral. Two uses for the price of one.

I left right after the kiss. I had lots to prepare before the final curtain came down. Married and widowed on the same day.

Chapter 12

T he Bright Brewery is booked for drinks and food. The staff there are more than accommodating to the guests. Not all guests stayed on because they had struggled to find accommodation for the night. All the motels, caravan parks, and B&Bs were fully booked thanks to the heavy snowfall they had that month. The Alpine Ranges are famous for the ski slopes. Suzi's dad paid double for the lodge; the lodge saw the opportunity to charge extra and they didn't hesitate.

All beer and cider in this venue has been brewed here. Sixteen different beers and four different ciders, each with its own unique taste. The bride and groom are doing their rounds, thanking everyone individually for coming. The parents of both doing their bit keeping the older groups company, making sure they're having a good time.

To the naked eye, one can't tell there's anything wrong between the bride and groom. The tension is hidden well, but building. Anthony doesn't know why, but Suzi is acting a little peculiar – suspicious the more accurate word. But Suzi isn't going to let anything slip, yet. She's waiting for the right time.

Anthony checks his phone, thinking he's heard a ping indicating a message has come through. He's right – it's a text from an unknown number. He glances around the room to see where Suzi is. She's with one of her cousins, temporarily distracted.

He unlocks his phone and checks the message. A picture has come through. His face hardens and turns red from anger. He's not happy. He needs space to think. He walks over to where Suzi is and whispers softly into her ear that he'll be right back. He leaves and goes outside to the beer garden. Suzi follows his movements with her eyes. Her cousin is talking to her, but her eyes are focused on Anthony. She excuses herself and makes her way outside to where he's seated. He's on his phone looking nervous.

'What's up?'

He's startled and almost drops his phone. 'Oh, hey. Didn't hear you come out.'

'What are you doing out here?'

'Um … just taking a break. It's a lot quieter out here. This fresh air is great, isn't it?'

'What's going on, Anthony?'

With that tone he knows better. He needs to be careful how he's going to answer that question. Should he tell her the truth? This is what a marriage is all about, right? Being truthful to one another. It was in the vows. But he can't be honest about this. Not yet. *Give it time*, he thinks. He needs to lie, a little white lie. He promises himself from now on, after this lie, he won't lie ever again. He'll be honest to the core. He wants this marriage to work, and last. This will definitely be the last time he lies. Cross my heart and hope to die, or something like that.

'All good, babe. Let's go in and finish our rounds. I love you.'

They exchange an uncomfortable look, then Anthony makes the move. He grabs her hand and leads her back in. Everyone is being loud and happy and having a great time – everyone except the married couple. They continue socialising, giving their heartfelt thanks to all the remaining guests. If only the guests knew what was really brewing.

The last of the guests are making their way through the venue gingerly towards the exit. Luckily for most, their accommodation is within walking distance. The walk and fresh air will do them good.

The bridal party has a longer journey, though. The limousine is parked out the front and waiting for them to finish up. The drive is going to take about an hour. Drinking in the car will void all boredom. They pile in. The door is shut and music cranked up. The party will continue all through the night.

They arrive at Arlberg Lodge on Mount Hotham. The caretaker is there waiting for their arrival. He has final instructions to pass on to them before he leaves for the weekend. The lodge stands on its own cliffside on a remote part of the mountain. The closest civilisation is about fifteen minutes away by car. They don't have a car there, so any emergencies will be troublesome. Suzi wanted it that way. No escape.

The limousine is scheduled to pick them up on Monday at 11:00am. At this time of the year snow is heavy. It gets to be fifteen below zero at night. Any attempt to do anything on foot without the proper snow gear will get them an early ticket to their grave.

The gang is stuck out there for two nights. Self-contained kitchen, laundry facilities, sleeping quarters with a woodfire heater and enough food and drinks for the entire time they're there.

The bags are removed from the car, doors closed, and they all watch the lights of the limo disappear into the night, heading down the slippery mountain. Bale, the caretaker, gives them the cards for the lodge and vital instructions that are written and explained in a booklet. He's in his 50s with a strong Slavic accent, like an ancient king. His dark strong features make you want to listen to him. He'd be great as a lecturer.

He speaks to them about the warnings and what they need to do in case of an emergency. His last words are, 'Good luck.'

How appropriate.

The party head inside to get settled in. The fireplace is lit and a perfectly even stack of wood is piled so high it almost touches the ceiling. It sits to the right of the fireplace. It resembles an oversize game of Jenga.

'Okay, let's take our stuff up to the rooms and meet back here in thirty minutes,' says Suzi. Everyone does what they're told – one by one they pick up their travel bags and scoot off. Gucci, Louis Vuitton, and Prada to mention a few brands. Each with its own character, just like their owner.

Suzi and Anthony have the master bedroom that overlooks the main slope. They would never have given up the chance to take this room. Suzi's defence would have been that 'Dad has paid for this, so I get to choose.'

Betty and Barti are sharing a room. One is more excited than the other. Barti just wants the weekend to be over so she can get back to her normal, simple life. Free from all this bullshit. After this weekend is done and dusted, she will end her friendship with Suzi. She won't have to see them ever again. She'll come up with some reason and stick with it.

Or, maybe Suzi might just drop dead. Get lost in the snow. She knows that sounds cruel but she'll be doing them all a favour.

Betty, on the other hand, is Suzi's loyal bitch. She would do anything for her. Do all her dirty work. Would she kill for her? Many would think she would. Barti wonders if Betty would kill herself if Suzi asked. That is so morbidly crazy, but possibly true.

Craig is sharing his room with Karina. Strangely enough, Karina was allowed to tag along, even though she wasn't a bridesmaid. She was given a pass, like a thank you gift to Craig. It was the least Suzi could do, seeing he did everything he was asked. Even though Craig despises his sister, tonight he feels a little grateful. He'll let his hatred slide for one weekend. She's out of the house when they get back home anyway.

George is in a room with Marlon. Anthony and Marlon have been mates since primary school. They did everything together. They even got arrested together. They spent one night locked up in the local copshop for theft. Nothing too extravagant like a jewel heist. No, it was smaller than that. They stole a car for a joyride when they were sixteen. Suzi had been with them on this joyride, but her dad had enough money and influence to convince the police she had nothing to do with it. Only two out of the three ended up with a record. Amazing what cash can do.

Julie is the only one who doesn't have to share a room. She is all alone and pretty pleased about it. Being the black sheep of the friends, Julie had been left out from most things because she was different. The trust was never guaranteed with her. Occasionally, she might find herself included in things, but nothing to write home about. Her hatred towards Suzi dates way back to high school. Something she had to overcome leading up to this day. She kept her therapy a secret, like a lot of other things. Some things are best kept to yourself. She's here today for her own reasons.

They all meet back downstairs. Barti is the last one to join the group. They pour each a glass of champagne and raise them in a toast.

'To the bride and groom,' says Betty.

'To the bride and groom,' they all repeat.

'Before we continue with anything else, we need to open that little surprise envelope you would all have received with the invitation. Did you all bring it with you?'

They all reach into their pockets and take out the miniature invite. All of them hold it in their hands, eager to open it. Smiles break out that light up their faces, the joy this little envelope brings to them.

'Now, you all know that this wasn't planned by me, right?' Suzi says. 'I had nothing to do with it. I'm excited because it's most likely been planned by the invite lady, like a thank you gesture. Isn't this exciting? So on the count of three we open it up together, at the same time, okay? We ready?'

Everyone smiles and says yes. They rip the flap open and pull out the card.

The room has the air sucked out of it.

Smiles drop, taken over by fear. They are all left with their mouths open. Someone is playing a sick practical joke.

Someone asks just that. 'Is this a joke?'

Suzi drops the card and begins to yell. Uncontrollable tears begin to flow as the rest of the group collect their thoughts, not knowing what to do next.

The note reads: *One of you will die here tonight*

Chapter 14

(Police interview: Karina Torino – 27 June 2023)

Detective Donna Zammit: Miss Torino, are you okay if we call you Karina?

Karina: Sure. Whatever.

Detective Donna Zammit: Thank you for coming in today, Karina. Can you tell us anything about the Hen's Night? Were you there?

Karina: No.

Detective Louie Taylor: No, you weren't there or no you don't want to tell us anything about that evening?

Karina: No, I wasn't there. I wasn't invited.

Detective Louie Taylor: Bullshit. You must have been there.

Karina: No, I wasn't. You can ask the others. She didn't invite me.

Detective Donna Zammit: I've got this one, Lou. So, where were you that night if you weren't at the party?

Karina: I was out with Craig. He wasn't invited out with the boys either. We went to Maccas and then came back to my place and watched a movie.

Detective Donna Zammit: What movie did you watch?

Karina: Godzilla vs. Kong. It had just come out on Foxtel. We stayed in and fell asleep on the couch after the movie. Craig got up around two-ish and he left. I went to bed after that.

Detective Donna Zammit: Did you hear anything about that evening that you would like to share with us?

Karina: I heard a few things.

Detective Donna Zammit: What did you hear?

Karina: That Suzi drank too much and passed out. She's saying her drink was spiked. I find that hard to believe.

Detective Donna Zammit: Why do you find it hard to believe?

Karina: Because, I know how much she can drink. She's a fish. She can drink most guys under the table. And if her drink was spiked ... then she deserved it.

Detective Donna Zammit: What makes you say that?

Karina: Because she's a bitch to everyone. She has pissed off way too many people.

Detective Donna Zammit: Has she pissed you off?

Karina: Yes. Many times.

Detective Donna Zammit: But you are still going out with her brother?

Karina: Craig is the nicest guy around. She treats him like shit, too. I feel sorry for him.

Detective Louie Taylor: So, you both cook up this plan to get her back, is that right? Your master plan to get rid of Suzi and blame someone else? It was you two all along, wasn't it?

Karina: No, it was neither of us. We didn't do anything.

Detective Louie Taylor: Yes, you did. It was a plan all along to end her marriage and ruin her life, wasn't it?

Karina: You've got it all wrong. We did nothing. You should look at Betty, her best friend. She was close with her. She was jealous of Suzi. She always came in second to her. If anyone wanted to hurt her, it would have been Betty.

Chapter 15

Frozen to the core once the shock settled in. Each looking at the person beside them. Who would play such a practical joke? Jokes are meant to be funny. This is not funny!

Anthony reads the note again.

One of you will die here tonight

'Someone is playing a sick joke on us. Well, it's not funny okay. Stop fucking around and own up to it.'

Anthony begins to worry. After the text he received at the brewery, he knows something is going on. *One of us is going to die tonight … fuck.* Who? And who is the killer? This could be one of Suzi's jokes, but would she stoop this low on her wedding day?

She answers that question herself. 'I know who wrote this note,' she says, scared and almost beside herself. 'It was *her*. She played this sick twisted joke on us.'

'Who?' said Anthony.

'The lady who made these invitations for us. She has made these extra little invites.'

'Why would she do that?'

'It's obvious. She's a boring fucking cow and she gets a kick out of scaring people.'

'She wouldn't go that far, would she?' asks Barti.

'How would I know what she's capable of doing? I don't even know her that well.'

'Didn't she friend you on Facebook?' says Julie.

'How did you know about that?' Suzi asks.

'You told us. You even invited her to the wedding.'

'No, I didn't. She was not invited to my wedding. I would never have done that.'

'She was there, at the ceremony today. I saw her in the back row,' says Betty.

'I'm going to ring her right now and get to the bottom of this,' says Suzi. She takes out her phone from her back pocket and searches through her contacts. They all watch with anticipation. Who is this invite lady? What has she done? Why is she so interested in this wedding? Has she done this before to someone else?

'I only have the store number,' she says.

'Try her mobile,' Julie says. 'It should be on the card she gave you.'

'Good thinking.' Suzi reaches into her bag and rummages through the contents before she lands her fingers on the card. She takes it out of the bag and holds it up towards the light. The card is glossy, not much information on there, but there is a mobile number. She puts the phone on loud speaker so everyone can hear.

'Let's see her get out of this one,' says Suzi.

'The number you have dialled has been disconnected.'

She hangs up and tries again.

'The number you have dialled has been disconnected.'

She tries again.

'The number you have dialled—'

'Fuck. Fuck. Fuck.'

Frustration passes through the air. The fear is overwhelming and the bright flames of the fire are beginning to resemble Hell. The devil is about to emerge from it and act upon his sinister duties.

'Try on Facebook?' suggests Karina.

Suzi opens up the app and looks for her. She was listed under the name 'Invite-Girl.' But nothing comes up. She looks through her friends list. Nothing under 'I'. She scrolls through the entire list. Nothing, it's like she has vanished from the cyber world. It's like she doesn't exist. Suzi also tries ringing the store as a last resort.

'The number you have dialled has been disconnected.'

'Are you fucking serious?' Marlon says. 'Who is this woman?'

'What's her name?' asks Barti.

They all look at each other for answers.

'I don't know,' Betty says. 'We never asked her. She just went by Invite-Girl.'

'Check the card,' Julie says. 'There should be a name on it.'

Suzi looks closely at the card for a name. Nothing. Who makes business cards without putting their name on it? Then Suzi remembers something. Something about the Hen's Night.

'That girl. That girl I saw in the toilet before I passed out. I said to her that I knew her from somewhere but I wasn't sure where. It was *her*. She left the toilet just before I collapsed. *She* must have drugged me.'

'But why you?' asks Craig.

'No one was in there when they found you. They only saw a smiley face made with lipstick on the mirror,' said Betty.

Julie reaches into her bag for her phone. She needs to call for help. She dials 000. 'My phone is not working. I have no coverage.'

They all check their phones simultaneously. Then the lights go out in the lodge. The power has been cut. The only light visible is the one flickering from the fireplace and the dimmed light from their phones. The group have been submerged into semi-darkness.

Their phones have no signal. Someone has cut all the power, which includes the Wi-Fi. The words hang from a noose.

One of you will die here tonight

Chapter 16

S creams, then a thump.

Suzi screams again as she drops her phone. The screen cracks when it hits the floorboards. Shards of glass scatter across the wooden floor. She moves back slightly so as not to step on it with her bare feet. Her toes are painted blood-red.

They look around for any sudden movement. Each one of them is a potential victim. Any one of them could be the killer, hiding a secret that could cause the group's end, or at least one member of it.

Punishment – all of this has to be about punishment. But what have they done to warrant this?

'The caretaker said something about an emergency call…?' says Anthony.

'Check the booklet,' Marlon says.

They look for the booklet in the dark. The phone torch lights up their path. They all start looking in different areas. Where did they put it? They split up to speed things up. Some go upstairs to check; others stay on the ground level. Julie clears the glass from the floor so there are no unplanned injuries.

A voice comes from upstairs. Suzi has found the booklet in her room. She makes her way down the stairs and flicks through it, using her portable pocket-size camp torch she carries for emergencies. She doesn't go anywhere without it – she hasn't told any of them she's afraid of the dark, not even Anthony, even after all these years. The bright torch helps her deal with it. She scrolls through it and comes to the part that talks about the emergency call. There is a secret phone that dials out to the office down the mountain. It's connected to a mobile. The secret phone is in the kitchen. Stored in the pantry.

They run in to the kitchen and check the pantry. It's there, hanging on the side wall. It's a box with a button, PRESS FOR EMERGENCY written on a sign. Anthony presses it. It rings.

A sound is coming from upstairs. A phone is ringing. But whose phone could it be? They all check their pockets for their phones. All phones are accounted for. Anthony and Marlon run upstairs. The sound is coming from one of the bedrooms. It's Julie's room. They go in.

The sound is loud and is coming from the cupboard. They open it up. There is a phone ringing in there.

Anthony answers it. 'Hello?'

'Anthony?' It's Suzi, sounding confused.

He looks at the phone. This must be the one that's meant to be down the mountain. Someone has stolen it from the office and has brought it to the lodge. They take it downstairs and explain.

'What do we do now?' says Betty. Tears begin to pool into small puddles.

'There must be some other way to call for help,' says Craig.

'I want to know how that phone made its way into your room, Julie.' The question from Suzi is directed with hatred.

'What? I don't know how it got there. I've been here with you the entire time. I was in the bridal party – how was I meant to steal the phone without leaving your side?'

'Fair point. No one has left the group since this morning,' says Marlon.

Fear is making them turn on each other. If there is a killer amongst them, finding out who it is will be challenging. No one will ever own up to it, even if cornered. They're afraid to point a finger at anyone in case they might be right.

'We wait it out until morning,' says Anthony.

'What if we don't make it through the night? What if we don't see morning?' says Suzi.

'We will. There are a lot of us here. Surely, they won't try anything if we stick together.'

'There might be someone in here with us. Someone could be hiding in the lodge, listening to what we're saying.' Barti could also be correct with her comment. What if there is someone in the lodge with them, waiting for the right time to strike?

They decide to search the lodge. It's not a big place. Two levels with a few rooms. They search in two groups, making sure no one is left on their own. Suzi, Anthony, Marlon, Julie, and Barti go upstairs. Craig, George, Betty, and Karina check the bottom level.

They check the rooms in darkness with only their phone torch for light. Suzi has her camp torch. Every nook and cranny. Every possible hiding spot. Clear. Nobody is in there with them. A sigh of relief comes from Suzi. She tells them they shouldn't drop their guard. Something could still happen and they need to be on alert. They're stranded out on the snowy mountain in a lodge with no electricity, no internet, and no way of getting off it without freezing to death. They have no transportation and no communication with the outside world. They're all alone.

Or are they?

They regroup in the open space by the fire. Huddled close to discuss their next move. Anthony takes charge and speaks first. 'We need to head down the mountain and get help.'

'Are you fucking insane?' says Barti.

'Hear me out. We organise a group to head out, make our way down the mountain.'

'It's a death wish, mate,' says Marlon.

'You're insane if you think that would work. It took ages to get up here. I, for one, am not going out there,' said Craig.

'I think we should stay put,' says Karina.

'Will you volunteer?' Julie asks Anthony.

All eyes are on Anthony. His face has hardened up. He needs to step up and take control. His reputation is on the line.

'Yes. I'll go, but I need someone else with me. In case I run into trouble.'

'You're not going, Anthony McColloch,' says Suzi, using her serious voice. 'We just got married. I'm not going to be widowed on my wedding day.'

'I'll be fine.'

'What if there is someone out there waiting for you?'

'There isn't. When I said that something might happen, I was referring to falling or slipping down a slope or embankment.'

'But you will freeze out there. We didn't bring any of the heavy-duty snow gear,' says Julie.

'Let's search in the rooms for some extra gear before we go for help. We have no other choice,' Anthony says.

'I'll come with you,' Marlon says.

'Me, too,' says George with a half-cocked smile. 'My life is so boring that this will spark it up with some excitement.'

They check the cloakroom under the stairs. There's snow gear, coats, jackets, goggles, gloves and beanies. Everything they need to keep warm out there. Heavy snow and below zero temperatures make the obstacle in front of them that much harder. They leave the lodge, and the rest of them pray.

Pray they find help before anyone dies.

Chapter 17

The door closes behind them. Closed off from the rest. The mission is to make it down the mountain and raise the alarm. They are attempting this in freezing conditions. They can already feel the warmth of the extra layers of clothing help with the descent down the unmarked, uncharted, unlit path.

They can barely see a metre in front of them. Their boots pounding in the freshly dropped snow. Darkness makes it near impossible to see and manoeuvre. Their only hope is the ground they walk on. They can feel the bitumen of the road under their feet. They're trying to stay on it and not veer off their path.

They're sitting ducks if anyone is after them. Waiting for them to make their move in the dark. A body can be hidden well in this weather. Only after the snow has completely melted would they find the remains, what's left of them anyway. Animals would eat the fresh flesh, keeping themselves alive for the long winter ahead of them.

The lodge is not visible anymore. They're in complete darkness now. The stars above looking so beautiful, considering the predicament they're in. That thought vanishes, only to be taken over by fear.

They've been walking for about thirty minutes when Marlon reaches over and grabs Anthony's jacket. The three of them come to a complete stop. There in front of them is a dimmed light. They all look at each other before approaching it with caution.

It's a car with its headlights on. The car's engine has died. They walk up to it and try to peek inside. Snow is blocking their vision. They wipe the windows. Still hard to see. It's pitch black in there. They try the door. It's unlocked. They open it and the interior light comes on, brightening up the inside of the car.

George yells and trips over his own feet trying to move back. What he sees in the car makes him scramble for safety.

In the front seat sits Bale. Dead. His throat has been slit from ear to ear. Dark patches of what they assume is blood is splattered all over the inside of the windscreen and dashboard.

The keys are still in the ignition. They try starting the car. It doesn't kick over. It's as dead as Bale. They search the car for a weapon, anything that they can use to defend themselves. They find an axe on the floor in the back, rope and a bag of tools in the boot. They'll send for help once they get down the mountain.

The thought of doing that is temporarily put on hold. A large tree is blocking the path. Stopping anything from leaving the mountain. It wasn't there when they drove up the hill. Something must have brought it down between the limo leaving them at the lodge and Bale making his way back to civilisation. Someone definitely doesn't want them to get off this mountain.

The tree is too wide to jump over it, and, too long and dangerous to pass around it. They're stuck there now. Nowhere to go but back up to the lodge.

The girls place some logs on the fire, trying desperately to keep warm. There is enough wood to last them until Monday, but the question is: will they live that long?

Suzi checks her phone for internet connection. Still no bars showing. It has just gone past midnight. The group are getting tired. Barti is on the recliner zoned out, staring into space, eyes half-closed. Karina has fallen asleep, head on Craig's shoulder, both sitting on the couch. He's staring at Barti.

Suzi notices that Betty is missing. 'Have you guys seen Betty?'

'She went to the toilet about ten minutes ago,' says Julie from beside the bookshelf.

'Do you want me to go and check on her?' says Craig.

'Could you please? We should stick close by.'

Craig moves Karina's head carefully and places it on a pillow. She's dead to the world. He makes his way upstairs using the light from his phone. The door to the toilet is open. She's not in there. He walks to her room and knocks on the door. There's no response from inside. He knocks again, then opens the door. The room lights up when he shines the torch from his phone, enough to see what's inside. The beds are empty. He makes his way to the balcony. You can see the entire bottom living area from the top railing.

'Hey, she's not in the toilet or her room.'

They all stare up at him in with disbelief. Karina is still asleep.

'Where could she be?' says Suzi. They all decide to go upstairs and look for her. Karina is left alone on the couch.

They go from room to room. They're all confused on how she could disappear from a lodge this size. They enter the master bedroom.

Betty is asleep on the bed. She's holding something. A shirt. One of Anthony's.

'BETTY,' Suzi shouts. 'What the fuck?' She nudges her friend, trying to wake her up.

Betty opens her eyes, confused. 'Where am I?'

'You're in my room,' Suzi says angrily.

'Your room? I went to the toilet, felt tired, and went to lie down on my bed, in my room.'

'Well, you're in my room and you are sleeping with Anthony's shirt, you little bitch.'

'What?'

'Look in your hands,' says Craig.

She does. 'I don't know how that got there. I swear I didn't take it. You have to believe me.'

'Get out,' Suzi says. 'NOW.'

Betty drops the shirt and gets to her feet, rattled by what's happened. Someone has set her up. She's convinced she fell asleep in her own room, on her own bed and with no shirt in hand.

There is a loud bang from downstairs. They rush to the staircase. Karina is no longer on the couch. She's not there at all. Craig hurries downstairs, taking two steps at a time.

The stack of logs for the fire have tumbled over. There is a breeze coming in from somewhere. They look around. The back door is wide open. Karina must have gotten scared and run outside when she didn't notice anyone there. She will die out there. It's freezing, below zero.

Craig runs to the back door. Has a look outside but can't see anyone. He calls out for her. There's no response. He needs to go out to look for her before she gets too far, before it's too late. He goes to the cloak room, hoping to find another thick jacket and shoes to head out into the snow. But what he finds is not a jacket or shoes; Karina is curled up in a ball, leaning against the back wall with her knees pushed up to her chest, head in between her legs, shaking.

He reaches in there and helps her up. She is as white as a ghost.

'Honey, are you okay? Are you hurt?' He holds her away from him with both hands so he can get a better look.

'I'm okay,' she says. 'I got scared.'

'From the logs falling?'

'No.'

'From what, then?'

'I heard the back door creak open on its own. Then I thought I saw someone come in. I panicked. Got scared and I ran and hid in the closet.'

There's another bang, this time it's coming from the front door. They're all standing together, ready, wondering what will happen next.

Suzi grabs the fire poker, ready to use it as a weapon. She's not taking any chances. She walks over slowly, puts her hand on the door handle, and glances back at the others. They all have the same look on their face. Panic-stricken.

She takes a deep breath, holds it in, and turns the handle. She flings it open with force and takes a few steps back, with the fire poker raised above her head.

There's no one there. She keeps her distance so there aren't any immediate surprises. They wait, not knowing who is out there.

The back door opens again. They all turn, waiting.

Then loud footsteps approach from the front door, and two large figures come rushing in, and collapse to the floor. Suzi's instincts kick in, and she whacks one of them over the head with the poker. A yelp escapes from the one she's hit.

He stops moving. He's out cold.

The other one rolls over and puts his hands up in defence. Pleading not to be hit.

'Hey, hey it's us! Suzi, it's us!'

Anthony is pleading for Suzi to stop. But who was with him? Who got hit? Three went out, only two came back. They roll the other person over and remove the ski mask. It's Marlon.

'Where's George?' asks Barti.

Chapter 18

(Police Interview: Julie Kanellis – 27 June 2023)

Detective Donna Zammit: Can I get you a glass of water?

Julie: Yes, please. With lemon.

Detective Louie Taylor: What about a cheese toastie while we're at it?

Julie: No, just the water thanks.

Detective Louie Taylor: It was a joke, Miss Kanellis.

Julie: Oh.

Detective Zammit calls for someone to bring Julie some water.

Detective Donna Zammit: Julie, can you tell me what happened in the lodge last night?

Julie: They got into an argument. Then there was shouting and screaming.

Detective Donna Zammit: Who got into an argument?

Julie: Suzi and Betty. They both said some hurtful things to one another.

Detective Donna Zammit: Aren't they best friends?

Julie: Yes. But something had happened before that.

Detective Louie Taylor: What happened?

Julie: Suzi received a text from someone. Her mood changed right after that. She became a different person, like she was possessed or something.

Detective Donna Zammit: Were you there when she received the text?

Julie: Yes. We were all downstairs. Worried about George. He hadn't come back with Anthony and Marlon.

Detective Louie Taylor: What do you think happened?

Julie: Does it matter what I think? People are dead. My friends are dead.

Detective Donna Zammit: It does matter. It could help us solve what really happened in the lodge.

Julie: I think Anthony and Marlon killed George.

Detective Louie Taylor: What makes you say that?

Julie: Because of what Marlon had said.

Detective Donna Zammit: What did he say, Miss Kanellis?

Julie: That George knew what had happened with Anthony and that girl.

Detective Donna Zammit: What girl are you talking about?

Julie: The invite girl.

Detective Louie Taylor: Who is this invite girl?

Chapter 19

Marlon has come around and is now resting in his room. The disturbing sound of metal to skull was just that, disturbing. It sounded like breaking chicken bones when you're ripping a piece off the carcass. Crunching.

George is still missing. His chances of surviving out in the blizzard are slim, death inevitable as the minutes go by. One minute he was there with them, at the car, and the next he was gone. Anthony continues telling the others about the car and how they found the caretaker dead in the front seat. How the tree had fallen and was lying across the road, stopping anything from leaving the mountain and anyone coming up. They were stuck there until daylight. They still have about five hours of darkness.

Anything can happen in five hours.

They need to come up with another plan to see them through the evening. Something that is solid enough that it won't crack. They need to unite together, or one by one could fall victim, just like Bale – and possibly George.

Without warning, every phone begins to ping; tunes breaking the monotony of thoughts. Hands dig deep into their pockets to retrieve their phones. The Wi-Fi has been switched back on. Messages are coming through.

This means one thing. Internet – they can call for help. The thought has Barti in joyful tears. She can leave this dreaded lodge and continue the simple life she once had.

Suzi and Anthony can start their life as husband and wife. They want to put a stop to whoever is doing this. The scare tactics are over.

Along with the Wi-Fi coming back on, so too did the power. The lights have come to life. Their eyes take some time to adjust, get familiarised once again with their surroundings. But as suddenly as it came on, the power goes out again. The internet is cut, and they're back to being isolated.

'What the fuck just happened?' asks Anthony.

The same question sits unanswered on each of the others' mouths.

'Someone is definitely pranking us,' he continues.

'Was Bale's slit throat a prank, too? You dick, he's dead!' says Craig.

'What if he wasn't dead? What if he was just playing dead? What if all that blood and stuff was make-up, prop blood? I mean, we didn't touch him. For all we know he could still be alive. He had access to the place, he could have left his emergency phone here. I mean, he knows where everything is. What if he is the one doing it?'

A scream comes from upstairs. It's so loud it could have woken up the dead.

Marlon is up there.

Anthony and Craig run up the stairs. Marlon is not in his room. They look around the top level for him, torch flashing left and right. They make their way down the stairs, but stop halfway when they hear a noise coming from somewhere above them. Everyone looks up.

Marlon appears on the balcony, holding his throat, gasping for air like he's choking. He's leaning on the railing, his eyes rolled back. Before anyone has a chance to move, he breaks out into laughter.

'Had you! You really thought I was choking or had my throat slit, didn't you?'

'Mate, are you serious?' Craig shouts. 'Why the fuck would you do that?'

'Just playing with you guys. There is nothing up here—'

His sentence is cut short. His life even shorter.

Someone comes out from the dark behind him holding a knife. The others don't have time or the presence of mind to yell. It is over within seconds.

The knife makes one continuous sliding motion across his throat before the knife bearer vanishes back into darkness. They appeared and then exited the scene, perfectly timed.

Marlon's body goes limp. His eyes glossy from the fire's reflection. His hands wrap once again around his throat, only this time for real. Everything moves in slow motion. The sound is lost behind the screams. Marlon slumps over the railing, breaking the timber, and comes sailing through the air like a skydiver without a parachute.

His body crunches to the hard, mahogany floorboards with a thunderous sound. Bones breaking, blood pours out of his crumbled body. His body falls still, a pool of blood spreading under him.

Iron is #26 on the Periodic Table, and is a main component of blood. The metallic smell of Element #26 is filling the air and their nostrils. His lifeless body is displayed out on the floor for all to see. Not even a miracle can bring him back.

Everyone goes into shock. Betty faints from all the screaming. The vision of Marlon falling is embedded into her head forever. Anthony moves off the stairs and walks over to Suzi. She's frozen, eyes glued to the body right there in front of her.

Earlier today, Marlon was in a suit, standing next to Anthony; smiling, happy, alive. Now, now he's spread out like roadkill. Dead.

The group is speechless. Too afraid to open their mouths for more than screaming. Not knowing what words will come out. They need to do something to survive or they will all die. There is a killer living amongst them. The killer is upstairs, somewhere. Hiding in the dark waiting for their next victim. Waiting like a trap-door spider for their prey to walk by. Snatched out of innocence.

They can't leave. The road is blocked by a tree. It's cold and they won't survive the temperature. If they miraculously do survive the weather then there's the element of a knife-wielding killer on the loose.

They cover Marlon with the throw rug that was draped over the couch. An hour ago, Karina had it over her; now it's over Marlon's corpse. They leave him there on the floor. No one is game enough to move him. Each with their own reason.

They move away from the body and back up towards the front window. The same window that would normally overlook the snow-covered driveway. The curtains are drawn shut.

Julie puts a few more logs on the fire to keep it alight, and keep the room warm so they don't freeze to death inside.

'What do we do now?' asks Karina. 'We need to do something. I don't want to die.' The fear is noticeable in her voice, just as there's fear in everyone's eyes. They don't want to die, either. If they do nothing, that might just happen.

There are footsteps upstairs. Someone is walking around. A door closes. There is a door that leads from the top level down to the outside. Metal stairs make that journey possible. That's how they must have gotten in. The sound of footsteps making their way down the metal structure.

'Quick, lock the back door, now!' says Anthony.

Craig is the quickest to respond. He makes it in time before the sound on the steps stop. The back door is now locked.

'I'm heading up to lock the other door,' Anthony says. 'You guys stay here.'

'No! Don't go up there, please,' says Suzi.

'I need to, honey,' he says as he runs up the stairs.

Betty runs up behind him, holding a log for protection. They both vanish in the dark. The sound of them locking the door is loud enough for the others to hear and know that they're safe.

Suzi realises she never checked the text she received earlier when the power had come back on. She fishes out her phone and looks at it. There's an abundance of new messages. She opens the last message sent. She doesn't recognise the number of the person who has sent it.

But she recognises the people in the photo. She looks around to see if anyone is watching her. No one is; all eyes are on the upper level.

Suzi puts her phone back into her pocket and makes her way to the kitchen. She opens the top drawer and pulls out a large knife. Then she heads to the bottom of the stairs, stops and looks up.

'Suzi, are you okay? Where are you going with that knife?' asks Craig, concern in his voice. He knows that look; he's seen it before. When Suzi gets angry, she has the Devil's glare. Keep out of her way.

'Suzi. Please stay down here. Put down that knife. You might accidentally hurt someone with it.' This time from Karina.

The words fall on deaf ears. She is not listening.

Anthony and Betty make their way back down, telling everyone the door is locked. From a distance, in the faint light, Betty looks a lot like Suzi. She's wearing one of her tops.

Everything starts to move in slow motion again. The group see it happen before it actually happens.

Anthony makes his way downstairs and meets the sharp end of the knife. Suzi drives it deep into his chest. The suggestion of Suzi being a wife and widow on the same day is set in stone.

Sirens are approaching. Help is on its way. But it could be too late. This nightmare is happening for real. The sirens are getting louder and closer. They must have gotten through the tree that was blocking the path.

Suzi steps back and lets Anthony fall to his knees. Looking up at her like he is begging for his life. His eyes pleading for her forgiveness. Suzi not in the mood to forgive. And she is not done yet – her eyes are set on Betty.

What has happened to Suzi? What has made her turn into Satan? What does she know that the others don't? She has flipped and lost her way. She is having a psychotic turn.

But one of them does know.

Craig unlocks the front door and pushes it open. He ushers Karina out, and the rest follow. Betty is left inside the lodge with Suzi. This is not going to end well for one of them. If you were to place a bet, the one with the large knife will win. A win-win for Team Suzi.

There are screams, followed by silence. Cries followed by silence. Echoes followed by silence. Then the silence is taken over by sirens. Three police cars and an ambulance fill the driveway. If only they had arrived ten minutes earlier. None of this would have happened. They would have all been alive and rescued.

The officers and medics attend to the group outside, checking to see if they're okay. Then Suzi appears at the door, bloodied, holding the knife in her hand. Blood drips from it. No sign of Betty. Presumedly silenced.

A voice cracks through the night from behind the group.

'Drop the knife.'

Suzi obeys. The knife drops onto the snow, turning that spot red. Police pounce onto Suzi with force. Dragging her to the ground before cuffing her. She is lifted and escorted to the marked vehicle. Placed in the back seat. Locked away for the moment, and most likely for the rest of her life.

Chaos and carnage on Mount Hotham – the state has never seen anything like this. Breaking news will be plastered over the TV and papers in the morning. Family and friends wanting to know if their loved ones are okay. Reporters trying to get the scoop, the story that will rock the state.

There will be heartache, pain and sorrow for the rest of the bridal party. Memories that will last for eternity. These thoughts won't ever go away.

Chapter 20

27 June 2023

I once asked how far you would go to ruin someone's life. My answer was all the way.

My intention was to forget everything that had happened at school. Put it all behind me and start a new life, become a new me. And it worked until Suzi made her way back into my life. The recommendation to visit my store triggered the other side of me. The side that has always hated Suzi and Anthony.

When I saw her in the shop, I knew I couldn't put it behind me. Something needed to be done.

It all started back in Year Seven. I wanted to blend in, be liked and loved by everyone. It began well.

Anthony liked me. I had seen him from a distance and thought how hot he looked. I wanted to know what his mouth tasted like, his soft lips, the smell of his skin. I had the hots for him. A crush that went beyond.

I knew he had a girlfriend. Suzi Dawson. Everyone I had asked had some passionate hatred for her. Some even wanted her dead. When I got to know the real Suzi, so did I.

One day I had gone to the toilet and I saw Anthony in there with his mate, Marlon. Anthony was staring at me with his hot blue eyes, telling me he wanted some. He whispered something into Marlon's ear and then Marlon left. Then Anthony had taken his penis out and waved it around like a wand. I knew what he wanted.

As I got down on my knees, the door opened and Marlon had come in and taken a photo while my mouth was open. By lunchtime the whole school knew what I was about to do.

My life was turned upside down. The laughs and looks I got were irreversible. My life died that day.

Steve's life died that day.

I forgot to mention earlier. I used to be a guy. My name was Steve. That is why no one recognised me. The only person who knows I transitioned is my twin sister, Julie. She helped me become the woman I am today.

When I told her my plan, she was all too happy to help. I got the wheels in motion and she steadied the ship. A well-oiled team, I say.

To be completely honest, I only killed one person. Marlon. The person who took the photo and started the rumours. The rest was left up to fate. Julie played her part, getting me all the information I needed.

She just had to get Bale out of the way. I don't blame her for what she did. It needed to be done. The big picture was losing shape, so he needed to be erased. Killing him was the only thing that Julie could have done to protect us. Protect the plan. The rest of the group will get over it, eventually. It was Anthony, Marlon, and Betty who paid the ultimate price. Oh yes, and Bale. Poor Bale. Wrong place at the wrong time.

Suzi was convicted for three of the four murders. Julie had placed the same knife that was used to kill Bale and Marlon back in the drawer. It had all four victims' DNA on the blade, but only Suzi's on the handle. Her sentence will be carried out shortly. The murder investigation of Marlon is still ongoing.

I was cheeky and edited one of the pics I took of Anthony and me that night we had sex in the car. I Photoshopped Betty's face onto mine, and sent that photo to Suzi when I switched the power back on.

I hope she gets a life sentence for every murder. A hundred years. Not bad for a night's work.

They found George's body that same morning. He died from severe head trauma. An accident. His injuries were consistent with a fall. He must have slipped down the embankment. Poor George.

Anyway. I'm going to leave you now as I have a coffee date with my sister. This is where this story ends. I finally have a life to live. Love you all.

Xxx

THE OSCARS

Chapter 1

Kostas

I definitely didn't see it coming. All my hard work over the last twenty-seven years in the film industry has finally paid off. A nomination for Best Actor, and an invitation to the Oscars – which is being held on Koh Phi Phi Island in Thailand this year. I'm holding the invite in my hand and still can't believe my eyes. It's all surreal to me.

I currently don't have a plus one, so I need to get cracking on choosing the right candidate to be seen attached to my arm. It can't be just anyone. They need to mean something to me, someone I've shared close intimate things with.

I do have someone in mind, and I have always told them they would be there with me if I ever got nominated, but we currently aren't together. Actually, let me rephrase that – we WON'T ever be together again as she, my ex-wife Nadia, has put it bluntly. She moved on quite promptly and remarried. Her new husband, Ronald, is an old friend of mine. A real slap in the face. More like a kick in the balls.

They own a chain of fashion boutiques called Braun. How original. It's their surname. Year Tens could have come up with a better business name, but hey, who am I to judge?

My marriage failed for many reasons. First and foremost, lack of sex. Months would pass without us getting physical sexually. I had forgotten what she had looked like naked. I blame myself for that. Away for work ten out of the twelve months in the year had brought strain and depression to our marriage. She was married to me, but I was married to the job. Isn't that the correct terminology?

I would come home from a day of filming and Nadia would be in bed. A stained, empty glass of wine on the bedside table showing her loneliness. I wouldn't even have the decency to cuddle up to her and give her a kiss on the cheek. What a sad excuse of a husband I was.

Another reason was communication. We never chatted. Argued a lot, but never just talked. There's a big difference. The times we did chat was all close-ended questions. 'Are you feeling okay?' or 'What time will you be home?' and the one that was asked frequently was, 'Do you still love me?'

Damn, that was a hard question. I knew deep down inside I loved her but was it enough to be married to her? I had left that question hanging on a hook, dangling there to be answered at a later stage.

Her mother had died a year before we separated, and I only had the decency to say, 'I'm sorry for your loss.' That's what you say to a friend, not to your wife. She needed comforting and love, two things I had no idea how to do.

I don't blame her for leaving, but I do blame her for leaving with Ron. I expected better from both of them. Not kick me while I was at my lowest point. But then I guess she expected more from me. It goes both ways.

Anyway, it's been six years since our divorce, but a promise is a promise. I can only ask, see if she wants to be my plus one. I already know the answer, but stranger things have happened. She might say yes, but Ron will say, 'No fucking way.' They have a four-year-old to look after now: Jemima Sue-Ellen Braun. The middle name after her mother. I guess she wanted her legacy to carry on to her daughter. I often wonder if we had had a kid together whether she would have called her Sue-Ellen? Best to stop thinking about it.

The invitation is so precious between my fingers. It feels so delicate, as if it could crumble at any moment like ash. I haven't stopped smiling since opening the envelope this morning. Hand-delivered by the organisation themselves. They had parked their silver Rolls-Royce in front of my house and walked up my long driveway.

I live in Eaglemont, a posh suburb in Melbourne. The price of houses here is higher than most of the other burbs. The size of the enormous house on an extremely large property makes the mortgage look somewhat normal. I bought this place five years ago, after our finances were settled. We used the same lawyer, a family friend of ours, which made things easier. We had a mutual agreement on the majority of the items. I yielded to make it civil. We walked away happy, dividing everything we owned 50/50. It was a win for both parties.

Now for the hard part. Harder than the day I asked her to marry me. I need to message Nadia and invite her to the awards in Thailand.

Wish me luck.

Chapter 2

Nadia

Jemima has no kinder today. I've been dreading this day for weeks. I received an email from kinder telling all parents that today, 'Friday the Thirteenth of October is a pupil-free day. Kids are asked to stay home.'

Great, that's just what I needed. I've been stressed as of late and this … well this doesn't help the situation. Ronald and I have had a few heated discussions that haven't ended well. All verbally – he would never lay a finger on me. We haven't spoken a word to each other in two days. I'm so used to the silent argument treatment, thanks to Kostas.

I've wondered sometimes during these arguments what he was up to – Kostas, that is. We've been separated for seven years, six of those divorced. How time flies when you think you're having fun.

As an ex-wife, I do wonder whether he has moved on. Found someone nice and compatible. I'm not sure why I'm even thinking about him. We haven't spoken for ages, actually years. The last I had heard from a mutual friend was that his acting career was heading in the right direction. That was all he was interested in. His life was movies. Time away doing that is what caused our marriage to end. I fell out of love with the man I had fallen in love with.

He's a great actor. I remember when he had first started out in Waverley with John Orcsik and the TAFTA group. He was determined to be the best in his class. He rose with such solid, ferocious success. He tried stage theatre for a year but it fell through. His heart wasn't in it. On a screen was where he wanted to be.

Our marriage ended abruptly after an argument that triggered some unwanted words, words about my family. We said to one another that it was mutual but the reality was I wanted out and he just wanted to remain in a relationship that clearly wasn't going to work. It had passed its used-by date.

He was disappointed I had moved on so quickly. Just the look on his face had said it all. He was pissed that I moved on with one of his old buddies. Shit happens, I guess.

Ronald is at work today. I've stayed home with Jemima. I always stay home with her when there is no kinder. He says it's a mother's job to look after the kid. I get really mad when he says shit like that. *Equals in everything*, I say, *including our child*. Some days I feel like punching him in the nose but I know that won't end well for me. I have a few issues, mentally. Something I had brought with me into my adulthood, thanks to my teenage years. Something I have my dad to thank for.

I have planned a day out with Jemima. I promised her a new art smock for school and new paints for home activities. We are also having lunch at her favourite café down Burgundy Street. She loves the waitress there and Alessia simply adores Jem. Alessia has bright red hair and a contagious smile. Jem says she looks like a superhero and feels safe when she's around. Plus, she loves the lasagne there. I can never make it the way they do. I've Googled the hell out of recipes to find the best one, but fail miserably every time. Practice doesn't make perfect.

The drive there is peaceful. I put on a playlist with all of Jem's favourite songs. Spotify is the best app for playlists. She tries to sing along to the words she doesn't know, only to make up lyrics. That cracks me up laughing the entire journey. My precious Jem.

Alessia walks over and gives Jem a hug. They speak in a language only they know. When I was at school, I had something similar with my friends called Pig Latin. We would swap the first letter of the word with the last letter and hold an entire conversation. It was so weird, and I've tried with my closest friends recently but we can't get it right. I've lost my magic touch in Pig Latining. Not a word. I made that up.

No surprise when Jem goes with the lasagne. I go with creamed chicken and avocado. A bottle of mineral water to share to wash it all down. It's always loud in the café. People enjoying good company and excellent food. The owners are sitting on a gold mine here. I've never seen this place quiet.

Our food arrives as my phone vibrates with a loud ping. I search for my phone with one hand in my bag while I put a chip in my mouth with the other. My fingers touch the rectangle device. I pull it out of the bag and swipe right to bring it alive. I'm left with my mouth open, almost choking on the chip.

Shocked and frozen with disbelief. I never expected to hear from him.

Jemima looks over and I notice a changed look on her face. She is surprised to see me surprised. 'Are you okay, Mummy?'

I'm not sure how to answer that question. This is a great time to lie. Not sure how to explain it to a four-year-old. I answer like any mother would. I quickly swallow the chip half-chewed, feeling it scrape the sides of my throat on the way down and answer her question.

'Of course, sweet pea. Mummy is always okay.' A smile seals the answer. Jem looks at the piece of paper Alessia had brought over to her earlier with crayons. She always knows how to keep my Jem occupied.

Now, back to the text. What does Kostas have to say? I read with anticipation.

Hi Nads,

I hope you are well and I haven't interrupted anything of importance. I have a bad habit of doing that from time to time :)

Anyway, I know it's been years since we have spoken so I'll keep it short and brief. I have been nominated for Best Actor for my last film and because I had always promised you that you would be my plus one, I was wondering if you would still like to consider that inappropriate proposal? There is an additional hurdle besides the obvious one. This year, it's held in Thailand and I'm meant to fly out in two weeks' time. There for two nights before flying back.

I couldn't think of anyone else and to be honest, I didn't want to share this moment with anyone else.

No pressure, but heaps of it.

Anyway, let me know what you decide, even though I already know it.

Take care,

Kostas

'What the fuck?'

I say it out loud instead of thinking it in my head. Jem was so occupied with her drawing that she didn't hear me say it, thank God, but the older couple on the next table did. I received a rather unpleasant look that would have brought the Berlin Wall down.

What do I do? He had always told me he would take me if he ever got nominated but I never thought in a million years he would ask me after we had divorced.

For the first time since I've known him, he has kept his word. But it is a little too late now. What will Ron say about it? He will freak out. Do I blame him? And furthermore, who would look after Jem whilst I'm away?

I can organise a nanny for the weekend. That won't put Ron out at all. But the fact that I'm going to the awards with my ex-husband is enough to drive Ron over the edge.

I can't believe I'm actually thinking about it. That's insane! *Stop it now, Nadia.*

The other thing I can't believe is that he called me Nads. He always called me that. I don't ever remember him calling me Nadia. Even at our wedding, he called me Nads. When he had read out his vows, he said Nads. Even during the speeches. Nads was normal, but now it's not so normal him calling me that. It doesn't feel right.

What do I do? I need to think about it before I message him back. Maybe I should let him wait a few days, before responding with my answer of 'NO.'

I receive another text. This time from Ron.

> Where the fuck are you? I've come home for lunch and there is nothing to eat in the house. Surely you can do some grocery shopping. You're not an invalid. Ffs

Decision made. I text Kostas back without any hesitation.

> I'd love to. Send me all the details.

> Nads

I'm going to Thailand.

Chapter 3

JR

The morning sun has broken over the horizon, and the day begins with a calm feeling around the island. Koh Samui is waking up to another day. The fishing boats can be heard in the distance, powering along the smooth ocean top while the noisy motorbikes bring the land to life. They outnumber cars 20:1. Kids as young as seven ride motorised bikes to school. The police here are paid to keep an eye on certain things, but their vision towards crime is another thing all together. The more you pay, the more they leave you alone.

The island is a large plantation. Coconut is the main cash crop here. Everywhere you look, it's all coconuts. The Samui prison is nestled amongst the trees. It's strictly a prohibited building – even driving past it could get you arrested. That is one place you won't want to spend any time in.

Tourists flock here all year round. Chaweng is the busiest part of the island. Lamai, Nathon, and Bophut are not too far behind. The main street has had a facelift over recent years. The Russians have come in and built strip clubs, attracting all the visiting Westerners. Millions of baht are dropped every night at these venues.

For me, this island has become my home. I've lived here for the last twelve years. I came out to Samui for a holiday with my mates and decided to stay. I run a little Aussie bar called G'Day.

I've climbed the ranks of the criminal chain in such a short time that I'm left the fuck alone and not bothered. My loyalty to the mob speaks volume and value. I come and go as I please.

Chaiyo is my right-hand man who runs the bar for me during the day. He's a loyal local who has earned his trust and stripes. The bar had attracted some trouble in the past and, on many occasions, it had gotten out of control physically. But in came Chaiyo, and all the trouble mellowed out. He has a way of talking to people. Humans have a tendency to listen when they have a gun directed to their temple.

'Good morning, boss.'

'Ahh, Chaiyo, my brother. How are you?'

'Good, boss. I go do job for you.'

'Yes, yes, of course. But before you do, we need to make sure we have enough supplies for tonight. Big night tonight, Chaiyo, big night.'

'I make sure enough, boss.'

'Did you tell that wife of yours you won't be coming home tonight? I need you here all night. Make sure we don't have any loud-mouthed pricks.'

'Yes, boss. Wife say understand. She good for boss.'

'Yes, she is. Yes, she is.'

We make our way around the back to check on stock. It's the first week of the AFL finals; Carlton and Collingwood are playing in the Elimination Final. We're expecting a huge crowd tonight.

We are at the back when I hear someone call me from out the front. I tell Chaiyo to keep at it while I go to see who it is.

I notice a tall white man with a long bikie beard, dark glasses like the ones Roy Orbison wore, and a haircut so close you would think he had been inducted into the Defence Force. Buzzed almost to the skin. With a face that rough he must have seen some pretty mean things in his life; most things he would have administered himself.

'Can I help you?'

'I want to speak with JR.' His thick German accent makes him that little more dangerous.

'Yeah, that's me. Who's asking?'

'I have a letter for you from Mr. Clive. He asked me to deliver it to you in person. He said he knows your response, so there is no need to contact him. Danke, auf wiedersehan.'

The letter is placed on the bar next to a tip jar, sealed. And just like that he's gone.

Jurgen Clive is an old associate of mine. I haven't seen him in over four years. A look of despair crosses my face. I wonder what Jurgen wants with me. I take the letter and place it in the safe. Whatever is in the envelope is going to have to wait until later.

The night unfolds as expected. The bar is full of loud larrikins, overweight dads, and horny young guns … or is it the other way around?

I've hired all the pretty Thai girls for tonight so they can mingle and stimulate the drunk men. Getting their dicks hard is a great way for them to dig deep into their pockets and spend cash. In return I give the girls their drinks for free and let them keep 15% of what they earn through sex work, which is huge in Thailand. Samui is one of its private burrows. The girls won't dare try and rip me off as they know the consequences. A few have tried but never have succeeded. A quick metallic facial with a knife makes sure they don't ever work in this industry again.

The beer is flowing cold and the guys are getting hot. The girls are doing what they're hired to do. The beer goes down so fast it stands no chance of getting warm. Singha and Chang beer are the most popular with the Aussie men.

The game is about to start. There are more Carlton supporters in here than Collingwood. This place could explode at any moment. A mark and goal would bring the house down. Heaps of foreigners are in here, too, choosing a team just by colour. Staying neutral as long as the beer keeps flowing.

I'm serving behind the bar while Chaiyo and a few of his Thai friends are keeping an eye out, waiting for someone to cross the line. Carlton scores the first goal and the bar erupts with cheers. Arms go up in the air and chests pump out like Foghorn Leghorn. So far, it's all going well.

From the corner of my eye, I spot an elderly man in the far corner by himself. He's wearing a long sleeve jumper, making the situation a little strange. It's over thirty degrees in here this evening and the heat is making him sweat profusely. The ceiling fans are circulating the hot air, giving it a sauna-like feel.

I look over to Chaiyo and guide him with my eyes over to the sweaty old man. He follows my gaze and wanders over to get a better look. He's now standing a few meters away from the old guy. My first thoughts are *suicide bomber*. My life and bar have been under threat before. This could be a scare tactic. A close watchful eye has been put into place for any sudden movements. It has been proven in the past how devastating these bombs can be. 202 people perished from the explosions at Paddy's Pub and the Sari Club in Bali.

It's half-time and the crowd begins to shuffle, most going outside to get some dense, polluted fresh air. The old man stays put. So does Chaiyo.

The bar is populated with bobbing heads and it makes it hard to keep an eye out for any sudden trouble. I watch closely, like my eyes are CCTV. A loud noise generates from behind the group of Carlton supporters. All eyes shift. Someone has spilled his beer and his mates are giving him a hard time. Boys.

The old man makes a move. He reaches for something under his jumper. I signal to Chaiyo to be ready in case. The old man's jumper comes up and over his head. He is standing bare chested. There is nothing under his top besides a hairy torso and a gut full of beer. He's harmless, and all eyes transfer back to the other patrons.

A young Thai employee is asked to look after the old guy. She'll spend the next half an hour with him playing the game Connect 4, get him to spend as much money his pockets are lined with. Treat the old man like a child to get what they want from him. Who would have thought of that?

A fight breaks out between a long-haired Swede and a Pom. They exchange some verbal insults before being asked to leave the premises. Their argument was over the other football game, what they call 'soccer' in Australia. They can take that crap out of here. There is only one football worth fighting over, and that's Aussie Rules.

Their posse follow the two out to the street. It spills onto the road. The police can handle it from there.

There is a sound of broken glass that comes from the other side of the room. The old man's temper has flared. He's arguing with the Thai girl. I catch a snippet of the conversation. He's upset because she keeps winning and he accuses her of stealing money from his pocket. I decide to look after this one myself. As the owner of the bar, sometimes it's best to deal with problems my own way. Coming from the boss makes people understand better.

I make my way over and whisper something in the old man's ear. The old man looks up and smiles. I whisper something again and this time the old guy gets up, and we both head towards the rear of the bar.

Stepping through the back door, I escort the old man to a bungalow at the back. It has a small window. The door a large padlock on it. I take out a set of keys and unlock the door. It's dark inside and we both enter. The door closes behind us.

The game is finally over and Carlton has won by four points. The majority of the crowd has left happy. The rest have to wait for the following year, hoping their team does better.

It's 4:00am and the bar has been cleaned, and all staff and patrons have gone home besides Chaiyo. He waits for his boss.

He doesn't have to wait long. I appear from the back holding a stubby with a cold beer in it and fashionably clean clothes. Showered and ready to sit and enjoy that same cold beer. Chaiyo sits with me, Coke in one hand and a cigarette in another.

I have the letter now, still unopened. I take out a letter opener and remove the contents. Words have been scribbled across the middle of a piece of paper. I scrunch it up into a ball, reach over the table and grab Chaiyo's lighter. I light the paper up and we both sit there and watch it burn to dust.

The few words that were written on the paper have set the scene for devastation.

Put the plan in place

Chapter 4

Kostas

I 've never liked driving in peak-hour traffic so I have organised an Uber to drive me to the airport. The flight I'm booked on is leaving at 9:00am. I'm running a little late as I had a script reading with my agent and producer the night before. They are casting the new *Superman* film, with filming to begin next year. The location they want to use is Geelong, out of all places. I'm thrilled it's close to home.

I'm dropped off upstairs at Terminal 2. I triple check I haven't left anything in the car. I pat my shirt pocket for my passport. It's there and ready to be stamped. I've just realised I haven't checked to see if it's expired. What an idiot I am if it has. I'll miss the awards. The one thing I've been waiting for my entire life is flashing in front of me. I flip it open.

Phew. Thank goodness it still has two years of validity. I look around to see if I can spot Nads. Not that it matters. The one thing I never had to worry about when we were married was her word. It was guaranteed that whatever she had said it would be done without question. I never had to ask twice. I'll check in and go through to the lounge to wait for her call.

I can see a few people walking towards me with their phones out, ready to take a picture. Fans, I can never get sick of them. It's great to be appreciated for your talent.

My suitcase weighs 21kgs. It's all shoes and shirts. My suits are with me on a hanger. I'll give them to the crew when I board to be hung upright. I better not forget them, otherwise I'll be going to the awards in shorts. I wonder if that has ever been done?

I hear someone calling my name. It's Nads. She looks great. I haven't seen her in years but she looks … great. I said that already. What's happening to me? Why am I feeling like a teenager spotting his idol and going to jelly inside? Boy, I better smarten up or she'll sense it on me – I mean *in* me – I mean … you know what I mean.

I give her a wave before she notices something more than what I'm feeling. Should I say hi? I should. It goes hand in hand with the wave.

'Hey, hi. How are you?'

'Yeah, better now I'm here. I almost didn't make it.'

What does she mean by that? Was she going to cancel on me? Cancel the trip, completely? I must look like a stunned mullet just staring at her. Please say something intelligent. Please say something smart.

'Don't worry,' I say with a smile, 'I would have told the captain to wait. That he wasn't allowed to leave without you.'

WHAT? What the hell did I just say? Did those words really come out of my mouth? How embarrassing. Here I am being nominated for Best Actor and shit like that comes out of my mouth. Look at the way she's looking at me – she's smiling and probably thinking to herself, *What a loser*. Kicking herself for even being here.

'That's cute. Is that what you would have told him?'

Oh boy. She's waiting for an answer now. But what if it's a trick question? Yes, or no? Which one is the correct answer? They can both be right and both be equally wrong.

'Of course, I would have. I need my plus one.'

She's smiling at me still. I think I saved myself. *Quick thinking, Kostas. Okay, no more idiotic answers for the rest of the trip*, I promise myself. *Idiot.*

I tell her that I'll go through to the lounge. She's spending some time with her sister, Laura. She is parking the car and coming in for a coffee. It's best if I don't hang around. I never got on with Laura. She had this mean streak to her that I didn't like. Something her three ex-husbands didn't like, either. I tell Nads I'll meet her at the gate.

Passport control is busy. It feels like I'm in there for ages. It's hot and stuffy, too. I have to remove my jacket because I begin to sweat. I hadn't noticed I'd dropped my passport while shopping in duty-free, but luckily a tourist spotted it. She tapped me on the shoulder and handed it back. My guess is she doesn't speak English.

My name is on the guest list in the lounge. MR. KOSTAS DELLOS in bold letters. I wonder if the winner award cards have been printed? Could my name be printed on one of them? Only time will tell.

I drop my bag on the soft recliner and head to the bar. A cold beer to get me into the mood and settle the flying nerves is necessary. Part of the nerves is knowing my ex-wife is flying with me, and I can feel a cold stab in the back from her husband. He's probably got one of those voodoo dolls in the closet, ready to prick and torture me.

Sadist.

The barman looks at me, surprised I'm ordering a beer this early in the morning. It's lunchtime somewhere in the world. Not here though.

I settle in and open my laptop to see if there are any details for the trip. I notice an email from my agent. I read it carefully and take in all the information. Someone is meeting me at Samui Airport to take me to my accommodation for the night. A boat out the next morning will take all the invited guests to the island for two nights. Invitation-only on the island for that weekend. The elite will have access to the resort for the time I'm there. This is going to be one hell of a weekend.

A lounge staffer makes an announcement over the PA to say they have just commenced boarding. Right at the same time Nads sends me a text saying the same thing. I better get going so she's not on her own for too long. I've never been thoughtful like that – and that's why it got me where it did.

I get to the gate in time to catch the end of the conversation Nads is having with her daughter on the phone. The last thing I hear is, 'I love you, Mummy.' For a split second it feels like I am still married to her. *Shake it off, Kostas.*

The look on her face tells the story of how much she is going to miss her daughter. I wonder if that story includes her husband? I hear my name being called for the second time today. It's a lounge staffer running towards the gate carrying something – my laptop. I had forgotten it in the lounge. That could have been disastrous. All the important information is on there. I would have been screwed without it. Someone from up above is keeping a close eye on me. Someone down here is, too – I catch Nads staring at me with a weird look. Her eyes piercing. I look away and head to the boarding readers with boarding pass in hand.

'Enjoy your trip, Mr. Dellos.'

I get that a lot. Every trip I take. They hand the boarding pass back to me and I slip it into my back pocket. Nads follows closely behind me, clearly thinking about something. Most likely her daughter.

We board and are shown to our seats. Business class with benefits. Extra legroom, larger TV screen, nicer food, drinks, and all the comfort you can ask for. We're seated in 3D and 3F. The middle two seats. The cabin crew are handing out hot towels to freshen up and crystal glasses of wine.

'Can I get you anything else, Mr. and Mrs. Dellos?'

We look at each other and smile. Neither of us want to correct them. Once upon a time it sounded great, now it just sounds dull – only because I know it no longer exists. For a moment we let it sit and go along with it. For the next eleven hours, Nads and I will unofficially-officially be married. I'm okay with that.

Then something unexpected happens.

Chapter 5

Nadia

My decision to go was made on the spot. I didn't have to think that much about it. After the text I received from Ron, I went home and broke the news to him. He was pissed and hasn't stopped whining for the last three days.

Mum is moving in to help with Jem. Ron will have too much on to even give a shit. He just hates the idea of me going away with my ex. I don't see the problem. Actually, I do, but he is just an ass.

Mum and Jem get along really well. They get on better than Jem and her father. Ron can be a little self-centred sometimes. It tends to be all about him. Jem gets given her colouring books and pencils and told to colour something in for him while he either watches the footy or does work.

Mum dotes on Jem. Makes her the centre of everyone's attention. My dad will be so grateful to have the house to himself. I bet he's down to his underwear, sitting on the couch, watching wrestling and eating Twisties. Dad will always be Dad, and I love him dearly.

I'm in my room packing my bag. I'm only taking a carry on with me. A few thin summer dresses and underwear. I checked up on the weather about an hour ago. Thirty-eight degrees. That's crazy good. I'm planning to buy something there for the awards night. Dress and shoes will set me back a quarter of what it would cost me if I bought them here in Melbourne. I'm a size eight, shouldn't be too hard. I can take something from my collection from the store, but why do that when I can go out shopping? Retail therapy at its grandest.

Little Miss has come into my room alone. She is standing next to me, watching me pack my bag. I can almost see that tiny hamster in her head spinning the wheel of thoughts. She tends to do that before firing out questions. But this time she remains quiet. Speechless for the first time. I wonder what she is actually thinking. I feel like asking her, but I hold back. What if she asks questions I can't answer? What if I don't want to answer them? She might think I'm leaving her and her dad for good and never coming back. Two days without her will be the longest I've ever been away from her since the time she was born.

I tell her I love her. She knows that, but she's not going to hear it for a few days so I repeat it. I tell her that I love her dad, too.

'I will never leave you my sweet girl,' I say to her.

'Will you ever leave Daddy?'

How do I answer that? I have no intentions on leaving Ron, but 'ever' is a long time. People break up all the time. I play it safe and tell her what she needs to hear.

'No, I won't leave Daddy.' I leave out the word 'ever'.

My bag is packed and my little princess wants to help me carry it down the stairs. I let her hold the handle and two percent of the weight. We walk down the stairs smiling. She looks so proud of herself and announces her help to my mum when we get down there.

Mum is looking at me with shaming eyes. She thinks I'm mad for going overseas with Kostas. Part of her knew my answer before I finished telling her the story. She also knows that I'm an independent woman and I've never let anyone dictate my decisions. Ron knew that when we first met. If anyone ever asked, I wear the pants in the family.

My Uber has arrived and is waiting outside. A glance is all I get from Ron. I walk over to him and kiss him on the lips. His breath smells of coffee. I tell him I love him and I'll be back in a few days. I also let him know that I'm just a plus one and would never do anything to jeopardise my marriage. He looks at me in a way that says I already have. I hug and kiss him while he holds Jem, giving her the same attention. A wave from mum and Jem sees me off as I head to the airport.

The Uber driver is playing one of his own playlists. It's Indian and I'm loving it. It makes me feel relaxed and drains away my sorrowful thoughts. I keep telling myself Jem will be okay. I know she will miss me as I will miss her. This is important to me; one day she will find out the value of keeping one's word. Nowadays one's word is priceless and is worth more than money itself.

It takes over fifteen minutes to get from the bottom of the drop-off ramp to the front of Terminal 2. I'm not looking forward to fighting my way through the crowds though. I have this thing about confined spaces and crowds.

I hope Kostas has booked us good seats. Economy can be a bitch to travel in sometimes. Screaming babies, overweight people with their fat hanging over onto my side of the seat, and old people who have fallen asleep, blocking your exit and you're too afraid to wake them to get over their wrinkly body and legs.

I hop out and begin to walk through the doors when fear crosses over me. I have forgotten my expensive camera in the Uber. FUCK.

By the time my legs think to move, the car has taken off. I'm left with my mouth open and tears forming in my eyes. Frustration of leaving my baby behind has finally caught up to me. I can't control the tears and they flow like a waterfall. A woman walks up to me and I think she asks if I'm okay. I just look at her.

Before I have a chance to explain I see the brake lights of the Uber. There is a God! He begins reversing slowly and I meet him halfway, running to the car with joyful purpose. I grab my camera and give the driver a hug. It surprises him and he leaves with a smile. I walk back to the lady and explain what had unfolded. She also leaves with a smile.

I walk in and notice the mayhem that awaits me. People everywhere. You can tell who is going on holidays and who is heading back home. I wonder what I look like? Do I look like someone going to Thailand to be a plus one for my ex-husband who is nominated for Best Actor? I bet I don't.

From a distance I see Kostas. I head that way and call out his name. He looks around and eventually gives me a little wave. I'm so nervous. Not sure what it is. Maybe because he's my ex-husband and my current husband is at home with our daughter and my mother … or because I still have feelings for him? No, I don't have feelings for him. I know I don't. We're now friends and that's all there is to it.

He is staring at me with lustful eyes that makes me feel even more nervous for being here. Luckily only for a few seconds, as that look subsides into thin air. Perhaps I had mistaken his look for something other than what it was. He tells me he will meet me at the gate. Perfect. That works fine for me.

Laura is here to see me off. She works for Virgin Australia and has arrived early with me for her shift to have a coffee before I leave, and she starts work. Kostas won't want to be there to see her. They never really saw eye to eye. I don't blame Kostas for that. He never did anything wrong. Laura, being the big sister, always looked out for my best interests, only thing is she got it wrong with this one. She always said he wasn't right for me and that I was making a huge mistake getting married to him. She was wrong. I made the mistake for cheating on him with Ronald.

She wants to meet at T4 for coffee. It's a bit of a hike, but the further away I keep her from Kostas, the safer it will be. She gives me her regular spiel on how wrong I am for going and I do my regular thing by not listening. I end up spending twenty minutes too long with her – I tell her I need to head off so I don't get stuck at passport control. But I get to the gate with time to spare. A trip past duty-free for perfume and Baileys has stocked me up for the flight.

They haven't started boarding yet. I might just message Mum and tell her we're on our way. I think about messaging Ron but decide against it. I don't want his smart-ass comments ruining my flight. I tell Mum to give Jem a kiss for me and I'll ring her once I land. I also tell her to ask Jem what stuffed animal she wants me to bring back for her. I miss them both so much already – Jem and Mum, that is.

An announcement over the PA lets all passengers know that the Thai flight has commenced boarding. I see Kostas coming my way, looking all fresh from the lounge. There is a staff member running after him holding a laptop bag. He also left something behind. I break out in a silent laugh. My phone rings and I see the ID on the phone: Mum. I answer it and it's Jem wanting to tell me how much she loves me. We speak for a minute until Kostas gets close enough to hear. I hang up and think about what I'm doing. I close my eyes and when they open a boarding pass is held up to my face. Not sure why he has two, because I already have mine.

We scan our boarding passes and mine beeps oddly. The young staff member with an over the top smile looks on the screen to read. Kostas hands over the second boarding pass and she re-scans it. This time the beep is positive. Kostas scans his and we head down the aerobridge towards the plane. We get to the door and out of habit I turn right. Today I stand corrected.

'This way,' I hear. I look over my shoulder and notice Kostas walking into Business Class. I almost die from excitement. I look again at my boarding pass in case there is a mistake and notice the boarding pass reads Business Class. I don't want to leave this wonderful dream.

I quickly turn around and march through the curtains into another world I had only dreamt about. This is so fucking awesome. I sit down in my seat. I don't have to jump over anyone to get out of my seat. There are no annoying kids in here and the Thai music is soft and mellow. This is going to be the best flight I've ever had.

I get offered a hot towel and a glass of red wine. I take them both without hesitation. Then I hear a commotion coming from behind me. It gets louder. Then suddenly something happens.

Chapter 6

JR

I wake up from a bad sleep. My thoughts cascade from the letter I received yesterday. It all seems like a bad dream. I'm still hazy from overlapping nightmares. I have to get out of bed and confirm the news.

It's actually happening, and thanks to my involvement I have no choice but to go through with it. This will go down as the single most barbaric attack I have ever participated in. Terroristic and savage. I know Jurgen too well. I know what he is capable of. He has a reputation to cause deadly havoc.

I often ask myself the same question people ask me. Why am I involved with a man like him? Jurgen and I go back quite a few years now. Fighting alongside him back then was the only way to settle a dispute. Nowadays, courts decide legally what fate is deserved. Gone are the days of rolling up your sleeves and making someone's face resemble a bucket of smashed crabs. You both walk away with your head held high, if the other guy is still conscious. One of you was better, and the other licked their wounds and prepared themselves for another day. It ended then and there, and nothing more was to be said.

Jurgen had grown up in a poor German family where stealing and violence got you what you needed. His dad was a standover man for the biggest crime syndicate in Berlin. It had never been reported or confirmed, but Jurgen's dad kept a book of all the people he had to take care of. Dead or hurt, not many still breathing, made their way into this encyclopedia of hits. Jurgen had found the book one day, confirming what others had said, but never risked opening it; not even for a peek. He was afraid his name might end up in that book one day, so to avoid that he closed the book and never dreamt of looking for it again.

The book eventually vanished, along with Jurgen's dad. Hans's body was never found. He never showed his face in the area again. Til this day he is not sure whether his dad is dead and buried somewhere with the book or if he had just moved on to another country, very far away.

Twenty-five years on and Jurgen has picked up from where his dad had left off. Some say he involved himself in this world of crime to find out what really happened to his dad. There's only one person who knows the answer to that question – Jurgen himself.

A text message comes through. A number is displayed on the screen that I'm not familiar with. I open the message and begin reading. I know exactly who it's from by reading the first few lines. Jurgen's spelling isn't his strong suit. No one dares ever correct him as they know what would follow if they tried.

He wants to meet up in Bangkok. Patpong, to be precise. The capital of the red-light district. Every sex worker in Thailand has worked there at some point in their life. It's worse than the Bangkok Hilton. The underworld is run by the police. Nothing happens unless the cops give the word. Jurgen and the police commissioner go back a long way, too. Brothers from different mothers. If you want someone gone or locked up, just ask Commissioner Tommy. He has been at the helm for over thirty years. He will retire in that position as no one is game enough to challenge him. Some have tried and have all ended up swimming with the fish in the deep blue ocean. You get my drift.

The flight from Samui to Bangkok takes less than an hour. Bangkok Airways is the only plane that is allowed to fly to and from the island. As they own the island, they have placed restrictions on other airline companies, granting no access to this paradise.

A car is waiting for me outside the terminal. Jurgen has sent his regular driver, Miroslav, to pick me up. Loyal and doesn't take crap from anyone. Straight shooter with his mouth and gun. I do what I'm supposed to do and hop in. We exchange a look and nod simultaneously. Miro is a man with limited words, but his eyes speak words in many languages. An accent thicker than his skull.

Thirty-seven minutes later the car pulls up at the rendezvous. The door opens and I hop out to a dense heat and loud honking tuk tuks. I caught the last flight out because Jurgen wants me to stay the night and discuss plans. Jurgen is planning an attack that will top the last one. The commissioner, along with his entourage, is already here. The Black Claw gang standing guard at the entrance. No one is allowed in unless authorised. No one allowed out unless given permission. Dead or alive.

I take the two flights of stairs up. Smell of urine and pot clouding the narrow-walled space. There is limited visibility. I get to the floor where I'm meant to meet the others. The guards at the door search me, a thorough pat down in case I'm carrying a weapon to knock off the commissioner or Jurgen. The thought has never crossed my mind. Fear won't let me, even if I tried.

The room is small and dark. Music from the streets below us vibrating against the windows. A muffled combination of cars, motorbikes, and loud voices bouncing off the walls. Jurgen stands up once I enter the room. Commissioner Tommy doesn't. He sits there with a cigar sticking out of his mouth, matching his smoky sadistic smile.

'My friend, JR. It's been a while. How are you?'

'Doing well, Jurgen. Living the dream out on the island.'

'Excellent. It makes me happy to hear that. You do remember the commissioner, don't you? Tommy will help me plan this stylish gala event.'

I'm not sure if that last comment is meant as a joke. I notice an envelope on the table. My name is written across the front. I'm not sure what the envelope contains. My guess is either money or instructions. My eyes are glued to the package, waiting for Jurgen to continue.

'You can take the envelope. Don't open it until you are back in Samui. Tonight, we celebrate. This grand event I am planning will make us known to every organisation around the world. This will put the Nazis back on the map.'

And there it is. The one thing I was afraid of. The reason he is planning such an attack like this. The damn Nazis. The stories I was told by my grandparents were heartbreaking. And before you ask, no, this is different. I'm fighting for rights. The previous war was for power. But I never signed up for any Nazi domination. I'm doing this for *me*.

I look around the table. Butts on seats that mean nothing to me. A single bullet can end all of this but I choose to play this game, for now. There are sex workers down on their knees, bowing next to the commissioner. Kneeling there like they're his pets, waiting for a command. Waiting to please the fat bastard. Perhaps my bullet will please more than I had ever anticipated? These girls will be free from slavery, but prostitution is the only thing they know. They have needs, a family to provide for. I don't want to be the one to take that away from them. But this is making me angry. I know I shouldn't say anything. I've learnt from a violent past to speak when spoken to. Nothing more, nothing less.

From the corner of my eye, I see movement. Jurgen has made his way to the back corner. He's received a call and has gotten up to take it. He ends the call abruptly. A sly smile creeps onto his face like he's about to drop some good news. Jurgen puts his arm over Tommy like they're life-long buddies and whispers something into his ear. Tommy smiles.

Whatever was said, he's made Tommy move that big frame of his. He grunts and mumbles something to the girls in Thai and stands up, exposing his barge arse. He kicks one of the girls for good measure, just to clear the way for him to pass. He puts out his cigar and waltzes over to the door. His bodyguards are just on the outside of that door.

'I see you soon, my friend,' is all he says. I know he isn't talking to me. We aren't friends. Jurgen gives him a nod and says to me that it's time to party.

Jurgen has an apartment in town. Top floor condo overlooking the Chao Phraya River. The hustle and bustle of river trade goes right through the evening until morning. So much of it being illegal; something I'm quite sure the commissioner has a hand in, too.

I leave via the same way I had come in. The stairs seem a little steeper than I remembered. Then I realise this is not the same way. I'm led up an industrial set of stairs. The smell of cleaning fluid lingers in the air. A recent clean could be the reason why. Probably a murder. I wonder who the victim might have been, but a voice brings me back to the present. A strong German accent speaking in broken English. I look around to see a thick-necked giant with a shaved head yelling at someone small and innocent-looking. The beast must be another one of Jurgen's local henchmen. He is hard to understand, but I catch the word 'rough'. It could mean anything. I look around, trying to figure out what he is on about. Nothing comes to mind.

Jurgen stops and looks past me, directing his stare to the German. He says something to him and turns back towards the front. He continues up the stairs, stopping in front of a metal door. The word EXIT is sprayed across the middle of it.

I hear Jurgen call out the name of the giant. Otto.

I've heard that name before. It was about three years ago when I was in Bali. The name Otto was thrown around many times. Many have fallen victim to his bad temper. The word that has circulated from my sources is that Otto butchered his parents and older brother to get into a Neo-Nazi gang when he was seventeen. The authorities didn't have enough evidence against him so the case was thrown out. He made his name by cutting the heads off his victims and putting them on stakes in front of the house they lived in for all to witness. He is the most brutal and sadistic hitman I have ever come across. Knowing that he is here and involved with Jurgen makes me want to shit my pants where I'm standing. Eye contact with this madman is kept to the bare minimum.

We walk through the metal door and I see there is a helicopter waiting for us. The engine kicks over and this bird comes alive. Jurgen, Otto, and I hop in. Once the doors are closed, the metal bird begins its direct take-off from the pad. From one building to another in twenty minutes. The city below us buzzing with excitement. Somewhere down there, there is someone being manhandled. Someone being raped, someone being molested, and someone being murdered. Bangkok never sleeps. If it does, it dies.

The chopper lands on the roof of the Shangri-La hotel. The rooftop party has begun without the guest of honour. A DJ plays music that radiates across the soundwaves. One night in Bangkok and the world's your oyster. Lyrics made famous by Murray Head that have travelled the globe and back a thousand times. Mike Tyson also brings something to the table with this song from *The Hangover*.

We hop out and walk towards the bar. The chopper takes off and leaves us there at the party. Jurgen says something to me that I can't quite catch and walks off with Otto. The obvious thing I should do I don't, but instead I walk to the bar and order a Tiger beer. I take a sip from the cold bottle and feel the soothing crisp liquid trickle down my throat, satisfying my thirst, easing my tension. I turn my body and lean up against the bar, eyes like a raider, looking around to see who's here. I don't recognise anyone besides a charming young lady looking out of place. The reason she looks out of place is because she's a reporter with the Bangkok Times. What is Louise Tamaraporn doing here? Is she working or has she been invited as a guest? Friend of a friend of a friend? Who are those women with her? Friends of the friends? I should go and say hi to her so she doesn't see me as an arrogant dick. I'll finish my beer and go over.

I hear my name being called out. The voice comes from my right. I look over and see Otto with his hand raised like he's about to ask a question. He tells me the boss wants to see me now. I should make it clear to him that Jurgen is his boss, not mine.

I walk through some double doors that are opened wide and held open by sand bags. The wind can get a bit crazy up here, so these sand bags act as stabilisers. The room is smoky and filled with ugly men in suits. Average age of about sixty. The room smells of body odour and cigarettes. Cheap aftershave with a splash of pollution. I don't know who these guys are. One of them looks terrified, a short, fat man with stains on his crotch. From this distance it looks like he's pissed his pants.

He looks scared as to what might happen. I understand why. Two heavily built men in camouflage gear are standing behind him with machine guns pointing to the middle of his back. A Thai man in a grey suit with a top hat is yelling something to him in his native tongue. Whatever he's saying, the short fat man is listening and crying. Repeating his answers in Thai. My guess, he's pleading for his life.

There is nothing I can do for him. Even if I tried it would be too late. I barely got through my thought when Jurgen takes out his prized pistol and shoots him in the head. His lifeless body drops like a bad habit. The sound of Jurgen's gun echoes through the room and vibrates in my ears.

The body is carried out of sight by some hired muscles. The mood is returned to normal. Someone's husband, father, son, or friend is not coming home tonight. He'll end up with the other lifeless bodies that Bangkok has taken. I keep my eyes sharp and my ears to the ground. I fear that one day that could end up being me.

I get waved to leave the room. Jurgen is in a discussion with the suits. The look on his face confirms his plans are moving in the right direction. He must have asked for me so I could see what will happen if I ever try and double cross him. He looks over to me and says something to the man next to him, his eyes still on mine. I can read lips but the distance is a little further than what I'm used to. I don't want to guess what he's saying in case I get it wrong. For all I know, he might have just organised his next hit.

Me.

I pretend to be calm, but my insides are preparing for the final march down death row. Butterflies turn into moths as they try to escape my stomach. Shit, maybe he can sense my mood, my thoughts, my death. *Stay calm, stay calm,* I keep repeating in my head. Sweat beads on my forehead. To the naked eye, it might seem like the weather has taken an effect. In reality, I'm shitting bricks.

'JR.'

Fuck. Jurgen is calling me. I'm going to pretend I didn't hear him. I turn around when I hear him call me again. This time I make my way over. I look to his right and notice the bloodstains on the floor from the fat guy who had his brains scrambled earlier. A remembrance of a once living being standing in that spot. Now just an element.

'I don't like it when my friends double-cross me. It makes me feel sad. I give them what they want and in return …'

He lets that sit for a while. I know exactly what he's referring to.

The evening is getting a little weird for my liking and accidents seem to happen when I'm feeling this way. I need to find a way to get out of here without anyone noticing. I look up to the ceiling. CCTV cameras are constantly watching everyone's moves. I won't be able to pick my nose or scratch my arse without the cameras picking it up. Waltzing out of here doesn't look like an option.

I excuse myself and head towards the toilet. Once again, I pass the blood on the floor. Why haven't they cleaned it up yet? What are they trying to prove? Fear keeps everyone in line.

I enter the bathroom not knowing what my next move is going to be. Rotting faeces stuck to the side of the bowl. There is only one cubicle. Not much to choose from. Not that appetising when my nostrils are filled with the metallic stench of blood. Maybe this is the remnants of the fat man's last shit.

I lock the door once I'm in here. Not the quietest place to think. The sound of laughter and music blocking my thoughts. I need a way out. My thoughts come to an immediate halt – someone has walked into the toilets. I hear the tap turn on and the water run. Curiosity has gotten the better of me and I want to see who it is. I look over the door. I see the back of someone in camouflage gear. It's one of the hired guns. He hasn't noticed that I'm in here with him. I hold my breath so I don't make a noise.

A million things run through my head. Eliminating him is on top of my thoughts. One less scumbag in this world won't make that much of a difference, but it's one scumbag that won't take another life, ever.

My actions move quicker than my thoughts and I flush the toilet. I have to get out before questions are asked. I unlock the door and step out. Camo man stares at me through the mirror. A cold look that could kill a normal person. Luckily for me, I'm not normal.

He switches the tap off and moves over to the hand dryer. The noise of the machine blocks out all other sounds. Then, without thinking it over, I pull out a knife and slowly let the cold metal warm up with his blood.

I don't have an option now but to leave and pray to God that the cameras haven't seen me leave. The beast Otto is fast asleep, sleeping like sleeping beauty. Only difference is no one is waking this beauty up, ever.

Chapter 7

Kostas

I don't think anyone saw it coming, besides the suitcase itself.

The person in front of us hadn't stored his hand luggage properly in the overhead locker. The door had opened and out came the case. I watched it fall in slow motion, but still didn't have time to stop it. It came crashing down onto Nads's tray table which had a glass of red wine resting on it. The impact flung the full glass off the tray table, soaring through the air, and making its final stop all over my bright white D&G shirt. It all happens so quickly, my reaction is seconds behind. My now-red shirt matches that of a crime scene. Death on a plane.

And a waste of a good red.

The crew works frantically to try to clean the mess. The owner of the bag had been in the toilet. It is only after he notices his bag on the floor that he puts two and two together and owns up to the chaos.

His apologies come fast and furious with regret. His American accent makes it all seem okay. That's what happens in movies. Once someone apologises, everything seems to be sorted. In this case, the apologies don't stop. I have to accept $200 for damages to shut this guy up. I can tell you one thing about the Yanks; they take things to another level. This has gone through the roof.

Before I know it, the captain has announced for the crew to shut the doors as he is ready to push back. The only reason I know it's called that is because I spent a short time working for a ground handler at the airport when I was younger. Push back, on chocks, thumbs up from the engineer when it's all clear to drive the aerobridge on, all comes flooding back to me. I never lost the lingo.

After a short taxi, we are second in the queue for take-off. I look over to Nads and she has a smile on her face from ear to ear. For a split second the thought of her smiling so ferociously is because she is getting away with me. Then that thought subsides when I remember she left me for numerous reasons. Also, that she is happily married with a child. Two days maximum, and she will be back at home with her family. The next two days, I need to make an effort not to be inappropriate and to remember she isn't with me any longer. Two days of being just friends. I know it's going to be hard, but it has to be done.

The plane straightens out on the long runway and cranks up the engines to a deafening sound. The scenery outside begins to blur as the speed and direction of the plane thunders down the tarmac. I always hated the feeling in my gut during take-off; it makes me feel like it is going to nosedive straight back down. I guess watching *Air Crash Investigations* and learning that most crashes occur during take-off and not landing doesn't help me right this minute.

The nose goes up and the back follows as the plane makes its climb up towards maximum height. I look around briefly at the other passengers. Some have their headphones in listening to something soothing, a look on their face that shows no concern. Others have their eyes closed, probably from fear. Nads is looking straight ahead, probably thinking about her daughter. There is no control of your fate when you have both feet off the ground and in a 200+ tonne piece of airborne metal.

Within fifteen minutes the plane has levelled out and the seatbelt sign has been switched off. People are allowed to get out of their seat and walk around the cabin. I can never understand why, as soon as the seatbelt sign switches off, almost every passenger gets out of their seat and heads straight to their carry-on bags in the overhead locker to take out things of no use. Why couldn't they have just taken them out before take-off? It has bothered me for years.

I can't believe I'm about to do what I have always questioned others to do – I need my book from my carry-on. Maybe I'll wait for a bit so I don't look silly. I glance over at Nads and she has closed her eyes, probably just to have a quick nap. I let her be. I press the button to let the crew know I'm wanting something. I look up and the light shines bright above my head. Within seconds a pretty crew member walks over and looks down at me with her beautiful green eyes. Her smile makes me blush, makes me lose my words. She is stunning. I look over to make sure Nads doesn't notice me stumbling for words, not that she would care anyway. I need to keep reminding myself she is here for a getaway and for moral support. My plus one.

I finally get the words out that I needed a minute ago. Something so simple ended up being so hard. I wonder if she sensed my hesitation? She must get it all the time. Older man having naughty thoughts about a Thai girl. Not that I did. I'm being honest here. Her name badge says May. Would that be her real name or just a name they call her in English?

I ask her for a beer and the local newspaper. The local newspaper is in English. I'm happy they have the Samui Post. She returns a few minutes later with my beer and newspaper. She asks me if my wife would like anything. I'm not sure how to respond. To play it safe, I tell her that Nads is my friend who is travelling with me on a business trip. May smiles, then bows her head and walks off. I watch her leave. She meets with another crew member and they speak briefly before they both turn and look in my direction. I quickly turn my head and look the other way like an embarrassed child. They were clearly talking about me. Nerves filter through me that make my paranoid mind sink a little further into my seat. There is no escape when you're 30,000-feet up in the air.

The can of beer is already opened for me. I take a long swig of it and place it down on the tray table. The beer is chilled to perfection. It glides down my throat like a perfectly flowing waterfall cascading down a mountain front. I stretch the paper out, making it easier to read.

'Drug Bust In Samui', the headline reads. Largest on the island in forty years. Twelve men taken down with the bust. I turn the page. A shootout between police and a couple of the Russian gang members. Both mobsters dead, as well as one police officer. Page 3 gives some good news – the mayor marries for the fourth time. I guess he hasn't learnt after the first three. As I flick through the pages, a story catches my eye that stops me.

A body found abandoned in a shallow grave by the side of the road between Chaweng and Nathon. A bullet wound to the head and six stab wounds to his upper torso. His teeth and fingers have been removed, along with chunks of flesh from the body, possibly tattoo identification. I can't believe shit like this still goes on. I know Thailand is a third world country, but I'm still surprised.

Along with the local Samui paper she has also given me The Age. The front page sends me in a spin. 'Murders on Mt Hotham'. A bride killed multiple people at her wedding, including her husband and Maid of Honour. What is this fuckin' world coming to? I need to focus on the happy times in front of me. I'm curious to read if they have anything on the awards in Thailand. Not to my surprise, there is a three-page write-up, and my face is plastered across half of one. I'm glad they chose a photo that brings out my not-so-youthful good looks.

Enough with the news. I close the paper and place in in the front pocket of the seat. I've just realised my beer is empty. I must have finished it while I was reading the paper and hadn't noticed. May walks past and I smile, holding up my index finger, pointing to the empty can with the other. She gets the hint and walks back towards the front, following my request.

The memory of the body found in a shallow grave in Thailand comes back to mind. Samui is where we are flying into for a night before the boat ride to Koh Phi Phi.

I look over at Nads, still asleep. Fear makes my heart flutter a little faster.

What if I can't protect Nads from danger?

Chapter 8

Nadia

That bag flew out of the overhead locker and landed square on my tray table. How the wine missed everyone else but Kostas is beyond me. He seems to be the unluckiest guy I know when it comes to unfortunate events; he attracts misfortunes like bees to flowers.

Clean up in aisle three is quick and efficient. The plane isn't moving until everyone is satisfied with the mop up and the passengers and crew seated. The checks are all done, the videos watched, and the demonstrations presented and executed.

I close my eyes for a second to think. I miss Jem so much already. It's the first time I'm going to be away from her this long. I know she's going to be okay. Ron is a good dad. My mother is there for back-up. Or is it the other way around? They have a decent relationship, Ron and Jem. I know I shouldn't worry, but as a mother it's something I can't help doing.

The plane begins to roar down the runway and I keep my eyes closed so the tears don't flow down my cheeks. I'm using my eyelids as shutters. Holding in the evidence that I miss my girl. I feel the plane lift. I know there'll be no coming back – for at least a few days.

Kostas bought me the ticket with the option to change it if things get a little stressful for me. The unbearable possibility of missing Jem or my baby not being able to handle me being away – even worse, Ron not being able to control and handle her tantrums and putting my mum under unnecessary pressure. So many reasons to fly back home with only one reason not to. The awards.

The plane is heading up. Feels like it's flying to the moon. Astronauts heading to space, circling the globe from above the universe, watching the earth spin down below. Looking out the window I try to spot my house, see if I can see Jem playing in the backyard. My silly thought sits there for a moment before I look out even further, looking to see her little floral dress flapping in the wind while she swings on the single swing hanging from the large gumtree out the back. The thought is wishful, delightful, but just that, a thought. We live nowhere near the airport.

I pull out my phone and begin to flick through photos of Jem and I. I'm submerged in happiness for that brief moment before everything vanishes from my thoughts as I get interrupted.

'Drink, ma'am?'

'Yes, please. Another shiraz, thank you.' *Or the strongest Bourbon in the tallest glass you've got* pops into my head. I smile because I'm the only one who heard that.

The first meal is served after a few hours in the air. I've always enjoyed plane food. A perfect number of servings of all delicious goodness. I've never flown on Thai Airways before and the staff are so accommodating.

Matter of fact, I've never been to Thailand, even though Thai food is my favourite cuisine. Pad Thai is the yummiest food ever made. I can eat it for breakfast, lunch, and tea.

We are spending one night in Koh Samui before we head to Phi Phi. Looking at the map of Thailand, I thought a plane ride would have been so much more efficient. But apparently the organisers have booked a boat to take all the invited guests to the island.

Nine hours later the captain announces the descent into Samui. I had dozed on and off the entire flight. I missed the second meal, trying my hardest to sleep rather than eat. I know once we land it will be late afternoon and I don't want to miss any part of the day. We are in Samui for only one night.

Samui Airport is small and has that paradise feel, just like Seychelles. A little carriage cart takes the passengers from the plane to the arrival hut. Kostas and I are in the front of the plane and first off. Pays to fly Business Class. First cart back means first to collect bags and head out to the beach resort. The bags arrive ten minutes later on a cart. I had decided right before I left to bring a larger bag with a few extra items. Plus I knew I would need more room to fit the extra clothing I'm going to buy when I'm here.

I spot my bag. It stands out from the lot. Bright yellow with green Christmas tinsel wrapped around the handle, leftover from the trip I took with Ron and Jem to Fiji. Memories come flooding in and I hold back tears, reminding me of how much I miss my baby girl. I make a mental note to ring her when I check into the resort.

All the bags get taken off the cart and placed in order of seating. A big black duffel bag has ripped at the seams. Clothes and contents are scattered. A large heavy-boned man claims the damaged luggage. His mates piss themselves laughing, having a go at his white jocks lying on the tarmac. I hold back a giggle. I look over at Kostas and he is off with the fairies, probably dreaming of his award and the speech he needs to prepare.

The resort we are staying in is the Chaweng Regent Beach Resort. I asked Kostas to book two separate rooms – it was part of the agreement. Being friends has its own rules and regulations. Our only connection now are the divorce papers stating we once shared a life together as husband and wife.

Large puddles are the only indication of a recent downpour. The sky above us is clear of clouds and no sign of rain. Not more to say about tropical weather, but enjoy every minute while you can. The resort transfer ride takes no more than fifteen minutes. We're greeted at the foyer by the staff who are dressed traditionally elegant. Pastel green uniform with a genuine Thai smile that could part seas. I love this place already, without having seen the rest of it. With hospitality like this, I wouldn't care even if I was sleeping on a pool lounge.

We hop out and the humidity hits us in the face like a brick. The air clogs my windpipe and makes me work harder to breathe. Lucky for us, there are no pollution-producing factories on the island that would make the air even thicker and harder to suck in.

We are ushered through the open foyer towards the check-in desks. The staff have all the papers ready to be sighted and signed. They recognise Kostas and greet him with an extra-large smile. The young female workers whisper and giggle amongst themselves. They have an actor in sight and that gets them all excited and flustered.

Kostas seems to be getting better looking with age. I try to remember what it was like when I had him in my arms, naked and rolling in our bed, making love. Or the passionate sex, rough hair pulling, and fingernail stabbing.

I stop myself. I have a husband and a daughter. I was once there but can't go back. I stop myself from thinking and come back to the present. I look around in case my thoughts had leaked and were too loud, see if anyone had noticed me steaming up behind my eyelids. No one did.

The ladies are still staring at him. I know what they see, what they are feeling. I stop myself and turn away. I move to the edge of the foyer. There's a stream that runs through the resort. Large orange and white goldfish swim freely from one end to the other. I glance a little further down into the resort and spot someone with an entourage. The first thing that pops into my head is 'another actor'. He has a posse following him like bodyguards. He is wearing khaki shorts and a summer shirt while his cronies are in business attire, ready to jump in if he's in trouble. He looks familiar, like someone I knew a while ago. Someone from school? I can't quite work it out. It's going to bug me until I do.

I jump out of my shoes when a police car with its sirens blaring passes by us. A vision of trouble enters my mind. But how something could possibly go wrong on an island this beautiful is hard to believe.

A hand grabs me softly that makes me jump again. I look around and see Kostas, with his gentle eyes and relaxed smile, telling me we're ready to head to the rooms. He has organised connecting rooms just in case I need him for anything. He also made it clear to me that the door in between the rooms will stay locked unless I want it open.

I don't want it open, and I'm a little annoyed he did that. It's literally ten steps from his front door to mine.

We walk in silence. I zone out and listen to the trees rustling, the birds chirping, flying from one tree to another, the chatting amongst the guests, and the sound of the ocean waves splashing against the shore. The sound takes me to another memory from a long time ago when I went on a trip to the Greek islands with my girlfriends from school. The best six days of my life. The long days sunbaking in the hot sun without a care in the world, the late nights drinking at the bars along the foreshore and the sexual encounter with Petros, the island stud. Memories that will stay with me forever. But that's all they are. Memories.

We reach the rooms and the front porch is cascading with ferns and island plantation. Greenery that makes the heart melt with joy. I look over to Kostas and he tells me we can meet at the pool in thirty minutes. Enough time to unpack, shower, and wear my comfortable, summery, island frock.

The room is clean and tidy and makes the ambiance of the surroundings more tropical than it already is. A slow burning candle with Thai essence slowly does its thing in the corner, creating a smell that makes my eyes close and dream a little dream. There is a gecko walking along the ceiling, and a smaller one on the wall the bed is pressed up against. Living and breathing this beautiful air, the same air I'm breathing. Jealousy creeps in. Jealous of a gecko. I smile at my stupidity.

I strip down to nothing and walk through to the bathroom. I turn on the cold water. Too hot for anything warmer. I hop in and close my eyes, and I let the water run free over my sweaty body. After a while I open my eyes and look outside the large window that overlooks the garden.

There's an elderly Thai man staring at me. Staring at my naked body while I shower. I scream. He smiles. I grab the towel and cover up. Too late. He's seen more than enough. He turns and continues working amongst the shrubs. He's the gardener with a wandering eye. Is there no privacy in this joint? Does this happen often? I guess he's seen many in the same vulnerable position. I walk out and get dressed. I make a mental note to check before I have a shower next time.

I leave the room and head to the pool. They have two pools at this resort. Did Kostas tell me which one to meet at? I don't think he did. I head to the one next to the beach. I'll wait there for him. The sound of waves crashing make me want to sink further into the banana lounge. My eyes close and I drift off for a minute.

I wake to the sound of loud screams and men arguing. I open my hazy eyes and I hear Kostas's voice. He is arguing with someone. I look over at the bar and notice the same posse I saw earlier, heated and violent jabs of fingers to his chest. I quickly jump up from the lounge and try to work out how to manoeuvre my groggy legs. I get there before anything more can happen. My first instinct is to jump in the middle and stop this nonsense.

Well, that wasn't a smart move on my behalf. What a fool. I get pushed over and land about two metres away on my butt. The pain shoots up my spine and makes me clench my teeth. I feel light-headed, like I'm about to pass out. I see someone walking up to me. My vision is blurry. I can't make out who it is. Their hand reaches out and helps me up. My body is numb. My vision comes back, slowly. The fuzzy outline becomes clearer. I see who it is.

It's the man I saw walking with his posse earlier. I look in his eyes. I've seen these eyes before.

It's Petros.

Chapter 9

JR

What are the chances. A million to one? A trillion to one?

This girl left a mark on me all those years ago. I remember her joy and passion for life. It was so long ago and it surprises me I still remember everything about her, but one thing eludes me. For the life of me I cannot remember her name. She mentioned it once in the hours we spent together in Mykonos – the island of love, the island of hope, the island with white buildings and ocean blue roofs.

Now to see her on a continent thousands of kilometres from where we first met has made me pause. My life has skipped generations to find me here, in Thailand, helping up the woman who taught me the most important thing in my life. Love.

'You,' I say. 'Mykonos, end of school trip with girlfriends, you …'

She is just staring at me. Fixated. 'Petros?'

She remembers my name. A lot has changed since then. But she has me feeling the exact same way she did all those years before, speechless.

We stare into each other's eyes for what seems like forever. I notice blood on her elbow. She grazed it when she hit the pavement.

'Are you okay?'

'I'm fine, thanks.'

Angelic. Her voice still sounds like it did when we first met. The letters capping each word with soft erotic sounds. That voice is embedded in my brain. Tattooed in my memory where I will take it to my grave. Do I still love her? I've thought about her often enough to ask myself that question.

Should I ask it to myself now? Will I answer yes? How truthful will my answer be?

I get shaken away from that with another question. A question not asked by her, but *him*. Who is this bloke?

'Hi, I'm Kostas. And you are?'

I know who he is. He's that famous Australian actor. Are they married?

'Hey, nice to meet you. I'm JR.'

'Well, thanks for that, JR. These guys seemed to …'

I think he has just worked out they're with me. I'm guessing that because he has stopped talking and has this confused stare. I need to fix this. Not draw attention to what could possibly become international news.

'I apologise for the trouble my men might have caused. They mean no harm at all.'

I look over to the two goons. 'Gentlemen, please apologise to Mr. Dellos and …' I look over and wait for her to mention her name.

Kostas speaks before she can answer. 'Nadia.'

Yes, of course. *Nadia*. Sweet, beautiful, and sexy Nadia. How could I forget that? I get flashbacks from the past screening in front of my eyes. The memorable moments we shared, the unforgettable time we experienced together, the heartbreak when it was all over.

'It's nice to see you again … JR. It's been a very long time.'

'Wait, you know each other? How?' asks Kostas.

I wait for Nadia to respond. Her version will be more acceptable than mine. Hers a lot more understandable. We both look at him in sequence, like we're made from the same mould.

'The trip I took after I finished school with my friends. I had met Petros—sorry, JR in Mykonos. We spent most days together. His friends and mine got along really well and we needed a guide for the island. Petros offered his services.'

My eyes are showing a different story that I think Kostas has worked out. My guess would have been the same if I were standing in his shoes. A friend? Guide? With benefits?

'It was a long time ago, Nadia. Life has swayed in many directions since then.'

I can't tell her the truth. It won't sit well with her. It wouldn't with anyone. The less people know, the easier it will be to break away with minimal affect. How can I tell her that I'm a criminal mastermind behind several terror attacks? A hired gun to silence the loud voices? That I'm the world's most wanted man according to Interpol?

This isn't something I can advertise on my resume, or tell people I have just met. I've had to break ties with my family because of my involvement. To them, I don't exist. It's like I was never born. The life I've chosen is not one to brag about. I have sinned and caused pain, fear, and hurt tears. I've ended the lives of many people, good accidentally, and bad intentionally, and that makes me a dangerous man.

But before I disappear from her life again, I need one night with her. One night to make up for the time we didn't have. Dinner and a stroll along the beach, and then I'm gone for good. I don't beat around the bush. I ask her to join me that evening.

'Yes. I think that would be lovely.'

Chapter 10

Kostas

The nerve of this guy. Who the fuck does he think he is? I can't believe he just asked her out, right in front of me. I could have been her husband for all he knew. I was once. She's here with me. As my date on this trip that I invited her on.

She is smiling and engaging with JR, or whatever his name is. I wonder what happened all those years ago in Greece. Yes, I know it was way before our time together but it's making me feel uncomfortable. If things make me feel uncomfortable, I like to talk about it. I wonder if she has registered how I'm feeling? Is it written all over my face like an allergic reaction? Surely she can see the steam coming from my ears, the slouch in my body? I don't wait, I need to say something now.

'We have plans tonight, JR, so you know what? Maybe another time.'

Did I just say that out loud? I must have because they have both turned towards me with a loaded look. Looks I have seen before when

167

Nads and I were married. The day I accused her of cheating on me with our neighbour, Stan, the kickboxer. Everything seemed to go downhill from that day. Looks like the spiral has commenced, again.

My blood stops flowing as I wait with anticipation for her response. Nothing happens though. Silence. That's not good. It never turns out well when there's a long period of time with silence.

Is this really happening? They are walking away! And left me here with the two thugs who worked me over.

Correction. They have left me here all alone. The thugs are following their leader.

She's not my leader or keeper. She is my ex-wife and now possibly my ex-friend. I have fucked things up, again. I notice the bar. I might just spend the day here. You tend to find other lonely people in places like this. A childish reaction deserves a childish punishment. Off to the naughty corner I go. I spend the long day alone thinking about my actions. Regretting everything I've said. Me and my big mouth. My feelings for Nads seem to appear every time she is around me. Automatic feelings that don't seem to be there when she's not around.

I do miss her. I miss more things about her now than I did when we were together. I know I've fucked up. What's the use thinking about it? Nothing can be done now. I've lost her for good and I can't accept it.

I need to salvage some of the day, from what's left of it. I decide to go it alone tonight. One night in Samui before our early boat ride out to Phi Phi. There's quite a few Aussie bars down the strip. I'll hit town to forget the day.

There's one bar that stands out from the lot. A perfect name for my not-so-perfect day. I enter the G'Day Bar. It's full of people, locals and foreigners. A bearded beast who reminds me of a Viking is serving. Forearms that would give Popeye a run for his money. An exact lookalike for Jason Momoa. The closer I get, the bigger he gets. He's huge. Built like a mountain. A smile that would slice an ice cube in half. Eyes that would melt butter. Okay, enough now. I guess you get the point I'm trying to make.

He has an accent. German? Austrian? Nazi? There's a massive swastika covering the inside of his bicep. A reminder to patrons, letting them know who he is and what he believes in. My guess he gets no lip from anyone.

A live band is playing cover songs in the corner of the bar, a group of ladies dancing on the spot next to them. *Khe Sanh* by Cold Chisel. It sounds so much like the original, you would swear you're listening to Jimmy Barnes.

The men outnumber the women 4:1. That's okay. I'm here to drink, not fuck. I see an opening in the bar and squeeze myself between a couple of old geezers and a lady receiving all the attention she requires from a group of drunk, horny blokes. Their brains are too small to realise they're being preyed upon. They also don't realise they're being a bunch of male genitals – dicks.

'Bourbon and Coke thanks, mate.' My standard drink when I'm drinking alone. Slow sipping liquid gold that lasts longer than a beer. In this humidity, if you don't down your beer quick enough then it goes warm and tastes like piss. True fact.

Aquaman passes me my drink and I make a slow turn towards the band. Four members make up the hard rock band who call themselves Meat Pie. My laugh is muffled amongst the hundred-strong crowd singing along to the song. It doesn't take long for me to join in the chorus.

It takes a little longer for someone to recognise who I am. But then someone calls out from the back, 'Kostas fucking Dellos!'

Heads turned towards me and my cover is blown. There goes my idea of having a quiet evening. Aquaman looks over and calls my name. Waves at me to come over. I grab my drink and do just that.

He introduces himself as Klaus Zatopek. German-born Polish national on the run and hiding in Thailand. Looking at him makes me wonder why he's on the run and from whom. I'm not game enough to ask.

He leads me to the back where there is an adjoining room with shelf upon shelf of bottles of booze. Beer and spirits stacked ceiling-high like a library full of books. No need to read a book on what's going on here.

There's a single bed frame in the corner with a dirty mattress on it. Must be used to snooze in between shifts. An elderly Thai man sits by the door smoking his lungs out. Reminds me of my mother. 90 and still smoking like she is in her 20s. His fingers are tightly gripped around the cigarette. Smoke clouding the exit to the room like a smoke machine at a wedding.

Klaus tells me to rest back here for a while. He will bring my drinks to me when I want. It looks safer back here. I doubt the old man knows who I am. I thank Klaus and he turns away, stepping through a makeshift curtain to the bar.

The old man looks at me and smiles. I count four visible teeth in his mouth from this distance. Years of reckless abuse and a combination of nicotine and other lethal substances. He starts talking to me in Thai. I can't understand what he's saying. I look around the room, hoping to see another person who will help me with the translation. I know there is no one else here but I do it out of instinct anyway.

He lifts the packet of cigarettes and flashes his not-so-pearly whites. He's offering me a smoke. I wave and say, 'No, thank you.' He sits there and jabs them towards me again, his expression saying, 'Take one, you rude prick. It's an offering.'

I take one so I don't disappoint him. He passes his own cigarette over to me so I can light it from that. I do so and pass his one back to him. It's been about six years since I quit the cancer sticks. Six years since my blood was able to flow freely without sticking to the sides of my arteries.

I draw back a large amount and realise what a stupid fucking mistake it is. The room begins to spin and my breathing reduces to nothing. My eyelids grow heavy. I look over to the old man and notice him laughing.

This is the last thing I remember.

I wake up lying under a tree, naked and not knowing where I am or what has happened. I try to get my bearings together to escape this nightmare.

I feel something leaning hard up against me. The faint light from the moon gives me a faint visual. It's the body of a man, also naked, and still asleep. His heavy body leans against mine, and he's crushing my ribcage. I try to push him off me but he's too heavy. I try again to no avail.

'Move, you heavy piece of shit, you're squashing my ribs.'

Silence follows my demand with only the sound of croaking frogs. I look over again and realise this man is not sleeping. This man is dead, and I know that because his head is missing from his body.

Chapter 11

Nadia

So much has happened in the last couple of days, but I never expected this. Petros was a memory that wouldn't and couldn't leave my mind. It was only a few days back in Mykonos but it has lasted a lifetime. A memory filled with laughs, adventure, and steamy sex.

I feel a tingle in my honey pot just thinking about it. His hot, sweaty body thrust against mine. His soft, smoky lips, his tongue sliding around inside my mouth like a snake, and his hard, fully erect cock inside my wet pussy, stimulating me from the inside out.

I need to contain my feelings. I'm a married woman now. I have a child. I'm with my ex-husband here in a foreign country, as friends, not as a dirty secretive couple, supporting him with his nomination. I am a good, loyal wife and mother … just with dirty thoughts.

One dinner with my old fuck-buddy won't hurt, will it? I don't want anything from him. Just a catch up and to talk about the lost years. Chat about what he ended up doing; did he ever settle down, get married, have kids? How did he end up in Thailand? So much to discuss in one night.

I need to keep reminding myself why I'm here – to support Kostas. I don't want anything from Petros. Or do I?

Stop thinking about it and get yourself ready. That voice in my head has come with me to Thailand.

I fish for my room key from my little carry bag. I unlock the door and step into the air-conditioned room. I throw my bag and key onto the bed and head for the bathroom. I check to see if the gardener is out there. He won't see anything different. My body hasn't changed over the last couple of hours. But my mind has.

I finish showering and dry myself while I search through my wardrobe for something nice to wear. My eyes land on a nice little number I bought before I left. An elegant, tight dress that hangs off my shoulders. Perfect for this occasion. The colour is what attracted my eyes towards it in the first place. It looked stunning on the mannequin. My first thoughts were that it would look great on me. The mannequin and I have the same slim figure.

A quick glance into the mirror reveals that I was right. Flat slip-ons to protect my feet from the uneven footpaths, and a light-coloured summery lipstick has me roaring and ready for dinner. And it is dinner, not a date.

I'm meant to meet Petros in the foyer at 6:00pm. My watch says five minutes to. I lock the door and head out. Tropical manicured paths lead me to the foyer. It's well-lit, candles and torches give it that breathtaking island look. Picture perfect. Like a postcard. I reach into my bag to retrieve my phone. A picture is worth a thousand words.

But my phone isn't there. I must have left it in the room. Too late to go back now. Petros will be here any moment. I'm not nervous but nerves seem to make me tingle a bit inside, if that makes sense.

I look at my watch. Three minutes past six. He's late. Well, not really late. Do a few minutes past the scheduled time go down as being late? Each would have their own opinion on this. I think it's fine.

I spend the next God-knows-how-many minutes watching couples hopping in and out of cabs. Some going to dinner or someplace other than their room, others returning from dinner, heading for a walk along the beach, or possibly back to their room. Who in their right mind would want to spend any time in their room when the whole entire island is a resort?

Okay, now he's late. It's 6:37 and I'm here waiting. The staff are all looking at me, wondering what I'm doing. I'm quite sure they're contemplating whether they should approach me or not. The look on my face has kept them away. This must look bad for Kostas. They know we're here together. Though maybe some negative thoughts towards him is good. He acted like a dick earlier.

Finally, the supervisor approaches me with care. He's a young, handsome Thai man with a million-dollar smile, taking the time to work out what to say to me. I don't give him the chance.

'Can you please call a cab for me? I want to go to the most expensive, elegant restaurant on this island.'

He turns and blows his whistle. Within seconds, a cab comes around the corner. It stops in front of me. He opens the door for me like a gentleman. The cold air from the air-conditioned vehicle hits my exposed skin. Relief from the humidity that I've been standing in. I hop in and close the door. The manager walks around to the driver's side and gives him instructions in Thai.

'He will take you to number one restaurant, madame,' he says to me. 'He will also wait for you outside until you finish. He bring you back. No pay. Hotel will put on bill. Enjoy.'

That smile sees me off for an evening that I will spend alone. I can't help but smile back. This evening hasn't worked out as I had expected it to but it's a clear indication that my family back home have something to do with it. Jem and Ron.

I will never know the answers to the questions I had planned for Petros and maybe that's for the best. I'm leaving this rock unturned.

Chapter 12

JR

She looks as beautiful now as she did all those years ago in Greece. Watching her from across the street is killing me, but I know I've made the right decision. As it was the same decision I had to make all those years ago. I need to make sure she is safe. Nothing good can come from hanging around me. She won't be safe and I'm not going to live with that if anything does happen to her. Goodbye, sweet Nadia. Some stones are best left unturned.

'Chaiyo? Drive, mate. We have a big night ahead of us.'

'Yes, boss.'

Tonight is my final night of freedom. There are a lot of changes to be made and I'm the one who has to make them. I have thirty men I need to address and instruct on our plans. Some might not make it back, but that's something they don't need to know. The more they know, the more difficult this could get for them. There's also a possibility we could lose men before we even begin. The less they know the better.

I'm surprised to see all the men here, ready and waiting. I can see Jurgen with Miroslav at the far end of the warehouse. Commissioner Tommy keeps his distance from the lot. His presence will make a few men nervous. If anything happens to any one of us, the show *will* and *must* go on.

I hear a racket coming from a group of locals to my far right. They're speaking in their native tongue, which I can't quite understand. I turn to Chaiyo for some translating support. He tells me some of the men have found out what is going down and they're trying to pull out.

The commissioner has now become involved. He's addressing them in Thai. The conversation gets heated. I hope they don't blow this whole operation. We have worked on it for ages. If there is one man I don't and won't trust, it's the commissioner. A loose cannon, dynamite with only an inch of wick.

Chaiyo informs me that a few of the locals are pulling out, quitting the operation. They don't want to risk their life with what could possibly be a challenging one on the island, and possibly put their families at risk if it all doesn't go to plan. I tell Chaiyo that there is only one way out of—

I didn't get to finish my sentence. The sound of gunshots echo loudly; my ears ring for many seconds after it. I run closer to the action to see three men lying on the floor with blood seeping from their heads. A hush surrounds the warehouse. My ears still ring from the shots. No one dares to speak. The commissioner has silenced the entire crew.

I watch Jurgen as a smile begins to unravel on his face. That sadistic smile he has become known for. A look I have promised myself to remove off his face before I'm done with life.

Commissioner Tommy begins to speak. Everybody is listening. Even the ones who don't understand or speak the language are listening. Chaiyo explains quietly what he's saying.

'Rule number one: No one leaves here tonight. Rule number two: We all have a part in this mission and *it will* be carried out. Rule number three: Refer to the first two rules.' He also mentions that if someone doesn't make it back, their families will be taken care of. A promise he has given; a promise I know he won't keep.

The bodies are taken from the warehouse, most likely to be dropped out to sea, fed to the sharks. No evidence means no crime has been committed. My thoughts are with their families. These dead guys don't get a second chance.

I make my way over to Jurgen. Miroslav stands close to him, so close you would think they were joined at the hip. Miro is riding Jurgen's wave. When you're as important and wanted as the German is, you need all the protection you can get. He's hated more than Putin himself. Even his own mother despises him for all the wrongs he has done. All the sins, all the bloodshed, all the chaos. He would rather die an unloved man than a man not wanted. Jurgen lives off everyone else's fear. The Devil himself has a special seat for Jurgen at the table in Hell, seated amongst the evil and crazy of past and future.

'Come take a seat here, JR, you must be tired.'

He has no idea how I'm feeling. For the second time in my life, I've had to step back from a woman I love. A woman who made me feel special. No other woman has ever touched me in the same way and here I am again – for her safety and protection, I have to take a backseat.

'Hello Jurgen. Miroslav.'

'I don't know about you, but I'm very excited about tomorrow. This is going to be the highlight of my life, wouldn't you say?'

'I couldn't say, Jurgen. It's your life, not mine.'

'Yes, it is. Miroslav, please go get us something to drink. Vodka?'

I shrug. 'Sure, why not?'

Miro looks at me and then his boss. He has trust issues and I'm not making things any easier by being here.

'It's okay, Miro, I'll make sure nothing happens to your boss until you get back,' I say to make him leave.

If looks could kill, I'd be dead. That look the Serbian gives me could sink the Titanic. *Fuck you, Miroslav. Go get the drinks, you lapdog fuck.*

'Sorry about, Miroslav. He can be a little overprotective sometimes. It is like having a grown-up child still sucking on the mum's tit. He is not the sharpest tool in the toolbox.'

'Shed, Jurgen. Not the sharpest tool in the shed, is the saying.'

'English is my second language as you know, JR. Thank you for correcting me, but don't do it again. I don't appreciate being made to feel stupid. I don't want to have to hurt you before our big event, do I?'

'I guess not, Jurgen. I'll keep my mouth shut next time.'

I know what he's capable of doing. He wouldn't do it himself. He never gets his hands dirty. He'll get one of his henchmen to take me out. I bet Miroslav is waiting patiently for that task. He can wait a little longer.

The commissioner approaches.

'Tommy, how nice of you to join us,' Jurgen says. 'Drink?'

'Yes. Celebrating always make me happy. Today, good day, no?'

'Yes, it is my friend. All your men ready for the celebration tomorrow?'

'Yes. Some no happy, but this one not coming now. I have a little accident with pistol.'

I can't believe they're laughing this off. I know I have said this before but I swear to God, once this is done, so am I.

'I need to go and get my men ready,' I say. 'We have a big task ahead of us. Preparation, physically and mentally, is essential. Please excuse me.'

'Of course. You must do what must be done. We cannot have any mistakes. It will be costly for everyone if we do.'

What can I say to that? Nothing. Nothing more can be said. I should nod to acknowledge that I've understood. The only thing I'm acknowledging is that I'm involved with lunatics. I guess I'm no better.

God help us all.

Chapter 14

Kostas

After the evening I'd had, I had to set the alarm to wake me up. A total of two hours of sleep is all I got. The boat heading for Phi Phi leaves at 8:30am sharp. It gets into Phi Phi at 6:00pm. The resort where the awards are being held is situated at the docks.

I left the blinds open last night. The sun belting through the window had me up earlier than the alarm. That gives me an extra ten minutes to walk across the road to the 7/11 for a coffee.

I wonder if Nads is up, and what time she got in last night. I wonder if she spent the night in her room or did she spend it in JR's?

I need to stop wondering about that now. It has nothing to do with me. Yes, I still care about her, but she's also with someone else who should do all the caring for her. The person who exchanged vows with her after she broke them with me – plus, she has a kid with the vow guy.

I'll buy her a coffee and drop it off to her, as a good gesture. No, I'm not checking up on her. Well, maybe I am.

Coffee in hand, I arrive at her room and notice the blinds are closed. She must still be asleep. This will be a good reason to knock on her door. To say good morning, give her the coffee – it will help in waking up and getting ready.

I knock gently. Twice will do for now. She has always been a heavy sleeper. I don't want to sound too eager. But I can't hear any movement coming from inside. I knock again, this time a little louder. Still nothing – no footsteps, no banging, no sound at all. I might ask at reception to give her a call. Looking down at the time on my watch, I see we have thirty-five minutes before the driver comes to pick us up.

I head to the front desk and I speak to the lovely young lady there. I ask her to ring Room 202, Mrs. Nadia Braun. I need her to be ready on time to leave. She rings and I wait patiently. Okay, I wait impatiently now. I can hear the phone tone ringing. She could be in the shower. Her coffee is now getting cold. Out of frustration, I have forgotten to drink mine, too. I toss them both in the bin. I ask them if they can open the door to the room, to make sure she's okay.

The young lady leaves to go and fetch the manager, Karapong. He escorts me back to Nads's room, inserts the key, and unlocks the door. He pushes it open and there it is – the thing I feared the most. She isn't there. All of her belongings are gone, too – but where? This is bizarre. She would have called me to say something if she'd left. I check my phone. No missed calls and no messages. I try ringing her. Nothing. Panic has settled in and my brain is thinking the worst.

I know she was upset with me. To be honest, she was really mad at me. Do I blame her? I guess not. I acted like a jerk and most likely embarrassed her. If I were a board game, I'd be *Snakes and Ladders*. Every time someone gets close enough to me, they would slide so far down it would be impossible to get back up.

I look at the time on my phone. I need to make a decision. I'll ring Nads once more. If there's no answer then I'll leave and hopefully see her at the pier.

I head back to my room. I feel butterflies doing nasty things in my gut and I break out in a sweat. Nothing to do with the weather. My heart is racing so fast it feels like it's about to leap out of my chest. And the reason for that is because the worst-case scenario just popped into my head.

What if she did go out last night and something dreadful happened to her? I don't think I'd be able to live with that. The guilt that I've failed to protect her. Her daughter will be without a mum and it's all my fault.

I need to jump into a cold shower. I need to cool my body down, because I'm literally burning up. The water hits my skin with force. I close my eyes and all I see is Nads. I hear a voice. Someone calling my name. it must be my conscience playing games with me – it's Nads calling for help.

I hear my name called out again. It's a man's voice. I switch the water off and throw on a robe and answer the door. It's a man in a driver's uniform.

'Mr. Dellos. Car ready. I take bag and wait for you. You need help?'

'No help. I'll be there in a tic.'

'Okay, Mr. Dellos. I wait at car for you.'

The driver's name is Pako. He's an older gentleman with a weathered face. Years of doing it tough. By the look of his face and skin, I can tell he's worked extremely hard for every Baht he's earned. I'm grateful to have him as my driver and I'm sure his family is appreciative to have him as the provider.

Pako knows the importance of getting me to the boat on time. He's a local and has lived here his entire life. He knows a quicker way to get to Nathon. We pass small villages along the way. Houses made from tin and boards. A sheet hanging over where a door should be to protect them from intruders. Not much security here. Kids are playing out the front. Some play with sticks, which could lead to something a lot more sinister later on in life. They watch the car drive past like it's from the future. Their life just hasn't evolved yet. It's a Third-World country. We underestimate what we have and take for granted the things we're given. I am one of those culprits.

We reach Nathon in record time. There are people everywhere. I hope Nads is one of them. The boat is larger than I expected. Something Donald Trump would play on. Or Hugh Heffner and his bunnies.

Pako unloads my bags from the boot. I hand him $100AUD. His eyes glow with excitement. He and I know that this amount will go a long way here in Thailand.

I glance over to the security ahead of the queue. Armed forces with guns, showing that they are not going to take shit from anyone. Cameras flash as guests arrive for their voyage across the sea. I see my co-stars arrive in style. Leslie Kara is up for Best Actress for her role in our film, *The Hillside Murders*. She looks stunning. The cameras flash as she struts her stuff. She is so good in front of them. A natural. The movie is up for four awards in total, including Best Film.

I make my way over to the organisers and pull out my invitation from my jacket pocket. My lifelong work has come to this. This Invitation puts me amongst the elite. I have finally made it, and nothing can take that away from me.

A tap on my shoulder startles me.

To my disappointment it's not Nads but my friend, Chip Longmuir, the director. Over the past ten years, Chip has directed many films and has won an abundance of awards. This film is no exemption. He is the favourite to take out Best Director. I chat briefly with Chip until my papers have been processed and my ticket to board the boat has been stamped. I glance around to see if I can spot Nads. There's a herd of heads that I can't see past. I ask the processing team if a Nadia Braun has come through. They check the list and tell me the news I didn't want to hear.

'No, she hasn't.'

Porters grab my bags and usher me through the queue to the foot of the steps. Paparazzi are doing what they do best, taking photos and annoying the crap out of you. But without them, tabloids and magazines would go bust. No one will know you from a bar of soap, and so for that reason, and only that reason, I can tolerate these hyenas.

I look back towards the entrance of the queue. I see faces I recognise but not the one I'm looking for. I'm trying to stay positive, to convince myself that she's okay. Safe and in no danger. She has twenty-five minutes before the boat sails. Then both she and I are on our own.

I know what that feels like, being on my own, but under these circumstances it's not a good feeling. You know that saying 'pulled the rug from under you'? Well, it feels like that – only the curtains have been drawn, too.

I board the boat and head to my cabin. I take the refreshing champagne that is on offer and down it in one gulp. I take the second flute without hesitation, and down that with the same speed. My body begins to warm up from drinking the chilled alcoholic liquid. The bubbles rush to my head. I needed that to calm my nerves.

Nads is strong enough to look after herself, but we're in a foreign country with foreign laws. I've seen first-hand what can happen if you don't play their game and pay attention. This is why I'm keeping my mouth shut, not ever mentioning my headless body experience-the one I had woken up next to. I don't want her waking up next to some stiff corpse. Or better yet, I don't want Nads being the stiff corpse.

I shake that thought out of my head and grab one more drink. I go out to the balcony and lean against the railings, staring out towards the mountains.

'Where are you, Nads?'

'Who is Nads?' asks a soft voice. Angelic and pure.

I turn around to see the reporter, Louise Tamaraporn. She has a badge on: Official Event Reporter. She's been chosen to report the ins and outs of this event. Good or bad, she has a reputation to report it and publish it in her own words. I also know the lengths she will go to, the lows she will stoop to in order to get her story. I need to watch what I say and what I'm doing at all times. She's the Medusa of the Media. Not my saying – I stole that one from another reporter who had crossed paths with her and fell short. Nasty with a capital 'N'.

'Hi, Kostas. Do you have time for a quick chat?'

'Nothing is ever quick with you, Louise.'

'Don't be like that, this time I will be quick.'

I don't believe her and it shows on my face. Nads always said I have a bad poker face. A look that can be read by a five-year-old. I blurt out the first thing that creeps up to the tip of my tongue. It comes out before I can stop it.

'I don't have time now, Louise. I'm waiting for my partner.'

There's my first mistake. It's like I haven't learnt anything over the years. *Kostas, you idiot.*

'Partner? Who is she, or he?'

Shit. '*She,* and you'll find out in good time. Enjoy the boat ride.'

Perfect time to scoot. Before I turn to walk away, I quickly look over to the crowd at the drop-off zone. Still no sign of Nads. No sign of said partner.

I head for the bar and leave Louise stranded. Another time, another place. Under better circumstances. I feel the burning sensation on my back from her stares. Not happy that she has been snubbed. My care factor towards her is zero. There are other things on my mind that I need to focus on.

I order a bourbon and Coke, but change my mind. Straight bourbon. I change my mind again – straight honey bourbon. I hardly ever order anything straight. The only time I do is when I need to think. Now is that time.

I hear the sound of the horn, followed by a screeching whistle. The boat is ready to depart. Right on time. The clock on my phone says 8:30am. I feel the engines rev up, and the boat pushes away from the dock. Everyone is on board, except one. The one who counts to me is not here. I convince myself she's left Thailand to head back home. I'll stick to that for now.

The boat straightens up and the speed picks up. We're finally off to Koh Phi Phi. I'll try to avoid any confrontations or conversations. I want to keep to myself. Have some quiet time for the next few hours. I don't want anything to distract my thoughts.

I hear a ping. A message has come through to my phone. Could it be Nads? I reach into my pocket and retrieve my phone. It's not her, but it's about Nads. It's Ron.

> Is Nadia with you? I've texted and called but there is no answer. Let me know ASAP

Chapter 15

Kostas

My life has just taken a tumble. The exact same way Jack fell down the hill and broke his crown. In this case it's my heart that's been broken, not my crown. Actually, shattered into a million pieces.

I've let something happen to Nads. I'm trying to stay positive, but it's a little hard to when it's been confirmed that Ron can't get a hold of her either. What do I say to him? How can I respond to his text and report that I haven't heard or spoken to her since yesterday afternoon?

I put the phone back into my pocket and forget about the text for the time being. Nads might contact me or Ron, most likely Ron before me. She might have lost her phone and can't get in touch with anyone. These things happen, you know? I've known people to lose their phone numerous times.

Or … maybe she's had a change of heart, sick of being married, sick of being tied down. Bought a one-way ticket and made her way back to Greece. Mykonos is where her heart and mind have been for a long time. Maybe she's taken off with JR. A reunion that was meant to work, this time.

I hear an announcement over the PA. The voice sounds familiar, but I can't quite place it. Like a word that sits at the tip of your tongue, his voice sits neatly at the tip of my brain. I've heard it recently, but it eludes me where.

An arm springs across my neck. It brings me back to reality. Another voice I know whispers in my ear. His hot breath makes my lobes sweat. I can smell the scotch on his breath. Stale, mixed with halitosis.

'Drinks at the bar, mate.'

It's Sam Baker, my stunt double. I hadn't realised he was invited. Some things still seem to surprise me, like how people keep reminding me how much we look alike. I don't see the resemblance. Some days I look in the mirror and don't even recognise myself. Like my eyes are in cahoots with my brain.

I have no choice but to follow Sam to the bar. His arm is heavy around my neck; I'm dragged along like a girlfriend who is resisting her drunk boyfriend. Feet dragging like I'm on death row, taken to the gallows. I recognise most of the people. A couple of guys help Chip up onto the bar. He stands out like dogs' balls. Bright pink shirt, unbuttoned in the front, ripped jeans that sit just under his gut. A gut that he's proud of. Years in the making, priceless. A portrait of it would stand toe to toe with the Mona Lisa.

Everyone has been shushed, asked to 'Let the man speak.'

He begins by thanking everyone for all their hard work on the film, many thanks to the actors and crew, blah blah blah. I stop listening at some point until I hear my name. Chip has asked me to come to the front and say a few words.

Fuck. I don't want to stand on a fucking bar and make a speech. For fuck's sake. I'm in no mood to speak to anyone. I hide my feelings and emotions alongside the fear and thoughts about Nads. Over the years I've become pretty good at doing that. Pushing it all to one side where nothing can eventuate from it. Locked behind a closed door somewhere deep in my head and heart. There's a lot of things behind those doors. None that you need to know about right now.

I make my way reluctantly to the front. Smiles and cheers encourage me from all around. A couple of boos from my co-stars, jealous they're not up for an award. I don't blame them. I would boo, too, but I know deep down inside the boos are a joke.

I place my hands flat on the bar and push myself up, lifting one leg up first before the other one follows. I straighten up and stand tall. To be honest, standing up here makes me feel like I'm King Leonidas, about to make his famous speech to his men of 300. Looking out to the crowd in front of me, there's not one person I can happily say I will go to war for, knowing that it could be their last day on Earth. Some are afraid of their own shadow, not to mention a sword or a dagger.

All eyes are on me. The man of the moment. The lead in the movie, the actor nominated for an award. I feel my mouth begin to open, ready to address this hungry mob when, from the corner of my eye, I notice a figure walk by. A familiar shape and size. My head turns. I catch the back of him. My eyes are fixated on the shadow that follows him. I forget where I am and what I was about to do. A cloud hovers over me. I look back at the waiting crew. Waiting for me to speak.

I don't. I decide to find out who that person is.

I jump off the bar and head in the direction he went. I'm being lured by his strong presence, not sure what to expect – or who. I hear boos as I run past the now angry group. Probably confused more than I am right now.

I reach the corner, not knowing what's around it. As I turn, I collide with someone. His massive frame knocks me off my feet. He's not fazed by the collision. He's a mountain of a man. A group of men, soldiers I believe, swoop onto me and pin me down. I'm guessing soldiers because of their uniform – army green with straps and stripes. Army boots laced all the way to the top. Pistols in their holsters. Looks like they're protecting someone.

I look up. I know who they're protecting. That large figure I ran into is now standing above me smiling, cigar in his mouth, looking down at his prey, larger than a predator. I recognise him from TV and the papers. But what is he doing on this boat? Is he coming to the awards? Something doesn't sit right, and doesn't add up. Something smells dirty.

Standing in front of me is Thai Police Commissioner, Tommy Jandocsuk.

Chapter 16

Sandi Pornthongin – 13th March

An explosion has rocked the auditorium at Ao Ton Sai Pier on Phi Phi Island that has claimed the lives of 46 people with over 200 still missing.

Local police say that the auditorium was hosting this year's Academy Awards. The event was broadcast to over 150 countries, all watching live.

Witnesses say that it was like 'something out of a movie! A loud bang and then instant smoke. The explosion was heard from Viking Beach many kilometres further down the coast. Smoke clouded the sky.' Authorities have the place secured, not letting anyone in besides rescue teams and paramedics.

Amongst the confirmed dead is film director Chip Longmuir.

We will bring you more as the story unfolds. If you have loved ones who were attending this event, a hotline has been set up to assist with any enquiries.

The number to call is +66 75 422 599

Chapter 17

Kostas

I feel battered and bruised, like an apple that has fallen off a tall tree. Defeated and deflated without a clue of what really happened. I'm lying on the ground, discarded.

The commissioner is holding out his hand, a gesture to help me up. He lifts me up with ease – like Superman picking up a crushed car.

He hasn't stopped smiling. The cigar still burns bright in his gob. He reaches into his pocket and takes out a hanky. He points to his nose with his index finger. I touch my nose. It's wet. I look at my fingers – blood. My nose tingles painfully.

He finally speaks. 'No broke. Okay?' He gives me two thumbs up.

The pain I'm feeling indicates it's broken. The shape of my nose between my fingers feels wrong. His henchmen let go of me. I nod and walk past them. I pass a mirror as I take off down the corridor after the figure and see my reflection. I look like the Elephant Man. I need to ask if there's a doctor on board this boat.

I reach the end of the corridor. You can easily get lost on board one of these boats. I look back to where I've come from. The commissioner and his men have vanished, like they were a figment of my imagination. My nose tells me another story.

The door at the end of the corridor opens up into the dining area. I walk through and look around. The room is full of celebrities and their plus ones. The industry mates and opponents rolled in to one room. For now, I'm looking for only one. The person I saw in my peripheral vision. He must be here somewhere. I had noticed he was wearing a white jacket. Unfortunatly there are so many others who are also fashioning the white jacket look.

That voice I recognised earlier is on again over the PA, letting everyone know there are dolphins to the left of the boat, in case anyone is interested. Once again, I try to picture who that voice belongs to. A waiter approaches me and asks if I would like a drink. He's looking at me like I've just gone a few rounds with Conor McGregor. I wave him off, but before he leaves I put my hand on his shoulder and stop him. He looks at me in surprise, like I'm about to throw a punch or something. I read his nametag – Jeff.

'I just need to ask you a question. Who is the person that just made that announcement?'

'Oh, that's the captain, sir.' He sounds uncertain, probably because of my nose.

'What's his name?'

'Not sure. I can find out for you. It's his first time captaining this boat. I've never met him before and I've been here for a few months now.'

'Where is the captain that usually pilots this boat?'

'I can't be too sure, sir, but I overheard some of the crew say he had fallen ill and this guy is the replacement. It's great to have captains on hand when you need them. They just don't fall out of trees these days.'

'Can you please find out who it is and let me know?'

'Will do, sir. I won't be long. Will you be right here?'

'I'll wait by the bar at the front. The one up on the top deck.'

'Okay, sir. I'll meet you there in about ten minutes.'

I need to get out of this room. It's getting too loud and I can't think straight. Anxiety comes trickling in. Great, a panic attack coming on, too. The last thing I need. This will throw everything into disarray and cause me to shut down.

The last time this happened was at work about four years ago. I received news, and it took over all of my feelings at the time. I shut down completely. A police officer friend of mine, Max, had been shot while out on patrol. A regular stop and search turned deadly. The driver of the vehicle pulled a gun and shot him dead on the spot. Half of his face was blown completely off. His partner at the time was behind the car checking what was in the boot. Once shots were heard, he pulled out his service revolver and started firing through the back window. The shots echoed through the night like New Year's Eve fireworks. The driver was later pronounced dead at the scene.

An inquiry had brought closure to the case and ruled it in favour of the two police officers. Max's wife and two daughters were compensated, but they'll never have him back. They accepted a sincere apology from the government and police commissioner, which meant absolutely nothing to them. She and the girls moved back abroad to the UK where his wife was born.

Max was my best friend. We met in primary school. On his first day at school he was bullied by Louis, the school prick. I stood up for him and we both got our asses kicked that day. That beating bonded us for life and our friendship grew to a brotherhood. I miss his love for life, I miss his laugh, I miss his heart. I miss him altogether. RIP Max.

I went through therapy after the shooting. It took me ages to get over it. I felt like I had no choice but to kick my panic attacks and anxiety in the guts and soldier on. So I did, and moved past all the challenges to get back to what I love doing best.

I make my way through the plethora of talented actors and directors and step up to the deck. It's a clear day, without a cloud to be seen for miles. The sun is hot but the breeze is cool. The speed the boat is traveling at makes the day picture perfect. Cruising for the next eight hours will be enjoyable and relaxing. My mind drifts to Nads. I wish she was here right now to enjoy this with me. Better yet, I hope she's safe and well, wherever she is.

I look around for Jeff. Fifteen minutes have passed. I'll wait another five. I actually wait for ten, but Jeff is still nowhere to be seen. Most likely he's been whisked away for work and can't get out to me. I see another waiter. I'll ask him if he's seen Jeff.

'No, sir. I haven't seen him since he brought the last round of drinks out. I'll go and ask the manager.'

The kid returns in two minutes. His answer surprises me.

'Sir, I spoke to my manager and he told me Jeff was asked to attend a personal request from a group. He must be below deck. Who shall I say has asked for him if I do see him?'

'Tell him Kostas Dellos is waiting for an answer. He'll know what I'm talking about.'

'Okay, sir. I'll let him know when I see him. Is there anything I can get you?'

I can ask the same from this kid, but it might be best to keep my request to a limit. I don't want to arouse any suspicion.

'No, it's all good, thank you. I'll let you get back to work.'

He nods like I'm an emperor or something before he leaves. I lose myself and stare out to sea. It would be great to have one moment of peace and quiet. My mind is racing a hundred miles an hour. *Slow down, mate.*

'Kostas.'

I'm sure I'm hearing things. The sirens of the seas have me hearing things that are not there. Am I going crazy?

'Kostas.'

There it goes again. It's coming from behind me. This time I turn around. I'm left standing there with my mouth open, my heart frozen. I'm not going crazy. I shouldn't be scared, either.

'Nads!'

Chapter 18

Nadia

I can tell by the look on his face he was genuinely worried for me. The smiling surprise on his face also tells me he's relieved to see me. A part of me feels sorry, the other part satisfied. He needs to know that we are no longer together, as a couple, but only friends. What I do in my life is my choice. All I need from him is understanding and respect. Leave the hard part to me.

Before I allow him to ask the question that has most likely bugged him this entire time, I explain the story the way he needs to see it. I don't sugar-coat anything. He is a big boy and he'll have to get over it, one way or another.

The moment I had realised I had been stood up, I needed to make my one night here memorable. JR ... no, *Petros* didn't show up and gave me no explanation for it.

After waiting for a long time, the manager organised a car and driver for the evening. He told the driver to take me to the best restaurant on the island. This was in Bo Phat, the top end of Samui. The drive was pleasant, and he took me through small villages where kids and adults alike were happy. Tears formed in my eyes that I couldn't control. How can these people, in a Third-World country, have so much less than us, yet be happy? I couldn't get my head around it. So much pain and suffering, limited clothing, no running water, diseases and polluted water, yet you ask anyone here, young or old, and they will tell you they wouldn't change it for the world.

The restaurant was nestled at the end of the pier in Bo Phat. The menu is predominantly seafood but they serve burgers and chips with nuggets, too. I say, if you're in a foreign country try eating local cuisines, and not something you would find back home. I ordered the seafood platter and the meal was amazing. I sat on my own, soaking up the rays and the smell of the fresh salty breeze. I felt at home, in heaven, and I didn't want any distractions. I closed my eyes and a part of me was transported back in time to Greece. A time in my life when the only care I had was which bar was I going to be drinking in the next night. I had forgotten about everything in this present life for a few minutes until the sound of a horn brought me back.

After being there for an hour and checking my phone multiple times for messages, I had decided to switch the phone off. Petros had ample time to contact me to let me know why he hadn't turned up. It was the second time in my life that the same man had done that to me. I made a promise to myself the first time it had happened, future relationships would never go down that same way. And here I am again, many years later, going back on my word. The only reason I did go back on my word was because I wanted to know why it happened the first time. Petros was going to explain everything to me. Well, his explanation didn't even have to be verbal. I now know it was him all along with the issue and not me. Things happen for a reason, and this reason is because he's a jerk and an arsehole.

I told the driver I didn't want to go back to the resort yet. The night was young and I wasn't. I needed to feel good about myself. I wanted to do something so outrageous that it would be frowned upon if anyone found out. The driver gave me a suggestion and I fell in love with the idea. I told him to take me there right away. He said the best one was in Chaweng, not far from the resort. Bonus, I could walk home once I got tired.

The main street in Chaweng was busy. People everywhere. Loudspeakers playing music, motorbikes tooting their horns. Announcements letting the tourists know where to find the best and cheapest suits. Ask any shop owner and they will tell you they have the best suits on the island. What a cliché.

The driver parked directly in front of the venue. I hopped out and without giving me any warning I get blinded by the bright neon signs flashing all its beautiful colours. The banner said it all: Best Ladyboy Show in Samui. Four gorgeous people standing out front, attracting the bystanders, convincing the tourists that this is the place to be. They are absolutely stunning. Their hair, dresses, makeup, an absolute OMG moment. All of them over six-foot tall, gorgeous long legs. I was in love. Not literally, but metaphorically.

After the show, I was invited to the dressing room. I had struck up a conversation with a few of the girls and they wanted me to stick around. I sat and listened to their life stories. The heartbreak of torn families and the struggle of not being recognised. Did you know that successful ladyboys are treated with the utmost respect and dignity? They're considered highly intelligent and loyal to their peers. A successful ladyboy can earn up to $1000AUD a night. More than average people make in a week.

We sat there for hours chatting, mostly me listening. I was invited to go back to their place of residence and meet the rest of the clan. We had a beautiful late snack of fruit and wine before making a decision to stay the night. Before I could do that, though, I needed to collect my stuff from the resort. One of the girls, who had changed back into her masculine clothing, drove me to the resort on her scooter. I entered the room and collected my belongings, which weren't many to begin with, and locked the door behind me. I deposited the key into the late-night checkout box and left.

'I guess it wasn't logged that morning,' I suggest in response to his confused face. 'I came early and boarded the boat. My invitation was all wet and smudged. The writing was faint and hard to read. An official at the entrance recognised me and believed me when I gave them my papers, the passport sealing the deal. Apparently I had been spotted with you and confirmed me being your plus one. These unfortunate events led me to pass under the radar so when you asked at the desk if I had arrived, the answer would have been no. It wasn't documented.

'I saw you from a distance when you boarded the boat. I was going to approach you at one point but the reporter beat me to it. By the look on your face, it seemed intense. I didn't want to interfere. The second chance I got was interrupted by one of your mates. He practically grabbed you in a headlock and dragged you off to the bar. I knew it wasn't the time to approach you so I let it go.

'An announcement came on letting everyone know there were dolphins in the water. I got distracted by the voice of the person over the PA. I recognised it. It threw me off and by then you had vanished.'

Kostas looks exhausted. 'I've had a rough twenty-four hours. I thought you were …'

'Well, I'm not dead, and I'm here now.'

'Would you like to have a drink? Something stronger than a tea?'

'I would, but first I need to get something straight.'

'Sure. What is it?'

'I don't belong to you, Kostas. Even when we were married, I still didn't belong to you. Now is no different. You are not my carer or guardian. I am here because you invited me and I can leave anytime I choose. I am not obliged to take crap from you, or anyone else for that matter. I am here for moral support as your plus one. I have left my family behind to be here for you. Don't fuck that up. What I choose to do in my spare time is up to me and no one else. And I don't want to be judged for my actions. I love you for who you are, but we are friends only. We once shared a life together, but that is it. Do I make myself clear?'

'Yes. I will not get involved in your affairs again.'

'Excellent. Now let's go get that drink.'

'One question. Whose voice was that over the PA?'

'Oh, yes,' I say darkly. 'It was Petros.'

Chapter 19

Kostas

Nads is safe on the boat. I can now relax, and get back to business going over a speech I have prepared – the just-in-case-I-win speech. Every actor has one in their pocket, ready. A priest carries a Bible, I carry thankful words.

It's nice to sit here and absorb the sun, the sea and sparkling wine. It's also nice to sit here with Nads and have her explain her whole evening. Being stood up is not a good feeling. I've had my fair share of those in my life. Not to mention, it's degrading. Someone not wanting to meet up with you after it was planned speaks volumes of that person. I've learnt not to let it bother me anymore. Maybe it doesn't bother me because I don't date anymore.

Another announcement blares over the PA system. This time it's a different voice. Nads and I look at each other. Probably thinking the same thing – was it really Petros she heard earlier? The announcement lets everyone know that we're approaching Phi Phi Island. I look out to the distance and see dry land. Maybe this is the feeling the dove had when it noticed dry land and returned with an olive branch for Noah on his ark.

Everyone around us begin to scatter. They must be heading back to their rooms to collect their belongings. I suggest to Nads we do the same. Be ready to get off this boat and head for the auditorium. We drain the last of the champagne from the flutes and stand to leave. A waiter arrives with a tray to collect the empty glasses. I ask him about Jeff. He says he hasn't seen him for quite some time. I thank him before he grabs the glasses and heads off. I make a mental note to chase that kid up.

The boat comes to a standstill at the docks. The auditorium stands grand in the distance in front of me. Lights are switched on to mark a special event being held there tonight. I can't tell from here, but I bet the paparazzi are all in position, waiting for the arrival of the boat like pigeons waiting to be fed at St. Mark's Square in Venice. Escorts in tuxedos and fancy hats push carts, waiting for the guests to disembark.

The gangway is placed in position once the boat comes to a halt. People begin to disembark in single file. Nads and I wait our turn. Bags in hand, we step onto the walkway and then step off at the ramp. I see a board with my name on it. We head in that direction. We're greeted by a young man named Vincent. He explains what's required and we follow him and his instructions.

I look over my shoulder towards the top of the boat where the captain sits, trying to get a glimpse of who is driving the boat. It's hard to see as the sun is directly in my eyes. I squint and put a hand up to shade the glare. From where I'm standing it's hard to make out a face. Whether it is Petros or not is hard to know.

We make our way up the hill towards the building with its bright neon lights. An amazing structure on a gorgeous island. I make another mental note to visit this place once all this is done. A holiday for leisure, not work.

I was right about the paparazzi. They're lined up along both sides of the red carpet. Too many to count, too many to avoid, all with the same purpose: capture the most amazing photos of the celebrities. Photos like these can fetch a ridiculous amount of cash. Something I might have taken up in my spare time, if I had any.

I'm wearing my Armani two-piece suit in navy blue; Nads a Braun design. It must be worth a mint. She looks beautiful in it and stands out over all the others.

Click-click-click and, 'Over here, over here,' is all you can hear as guests walk the carpet, some called by name, all looking their best in their own way. We make our way down until we're inside the foyer of the auditorium. Canapes and champagne served on silver platters. All the guests mingling before the show starts. Friends before the battle begins, foes after the awards are done. The gloves are off and the battle will shortly begin.

We're ushered into the seating area. Rows and rows of seats upholstered in red velvet coverings. Chandeliers lit, sparkling so bright you almost require shades to avoid blindness. A stage so large it can accommodate a 100-piece orchestra. A perfect location for these awards.

An usher points to the row. Nads and I make our way over there and plonk our bums on the seat. Comfortable. Not a surprise. Within thirty minutes everyone is seated and the lights dim. The stage lights up and the music begins. Within two hours I will know whether I have won the award I have worked hard for. I close my eyes and take a deep breath. The show is about to begin and my heartbeat has its own heartbeat. Nads places her hand on mine for comfort. Eyes still closed, I feel at ease. It's going to be a good night.

Chapter 20

And the Oscar goes to?

'Chip Longmuir, *The Hillside Murders*.'

The crowd erupts, jubilant, a standing ovation for the Hollywood director. His seventh award, his second for this film this year. Hollywood has seen many great directors but none who can compete with Chip. Many actors turn to directing when they want to have a break from being in front of the camera. Chip has always stood beside one. His voice echoes in the minds of many great movie legends. Too many to mention, all touched with the greatness that Chip possesses.

He's swarmed with handshakes and hugs, his wife being the first. Crew members from the film all get their turn. Kostas is the last to congratulate him before Chip makes his long walk up to the stage. The presenter for the award is last year's winner, Dick Murdoch, who hands over the prestigious award before he steps aside for the man of the moment. The crowd await the speech.

'Wow. It would be an understatement if I said I'm surprised. So many talented directors sit before me, and this thing here in my hand is awarded to me. I'm honoured.'

The crowd applaud loudly.

'First and foremost, I want to thank my crew, my team, my colleagues. Without you, this right here, would not have been possible. All the sleepless nights, the private chats, the long days, all worth it at the end. I got the best out of everyone and this, this award, goes out to each and every one of you. Thank you.'

The crowd goes wild once more. He is truly an icon of the industry and a gentleman at heart. A well-deserved award, which is what the critics predicted. Chip walks back to his seat. He leans over and tells Kostas that he's going out for a drink at the bar. He said he won't be long. Back before any of the other awards are given out.

Chip picked the perfect moment to go out. It was like he knew there was going to be an intermission at that moment. He's beaten the thirsty mob to the bar. Kostas looks over and tells Nadia that he's going to catch up with Chip and he'll be right back. She decides to go for a toilet break herself and reapply her makeup. Most of the other women will be thinking the same.

The foyer is jam-packed with people. A large group surrounds Chip to give him their personal congratulations. Kostas keeps his distance and awaits his turn. Sam Baker brushes past him. He hasn't stopped drinking from the moment the boat left Samui. He's a little wobbly on his feet. He stumbles towards the toilet, bumping into people as he passes. He enters as another two exit. Another man follows Sam into the loo.

Inside the toilet, Sam waits for an opening. It's busy in there, loud and lots of chatter, like a market in Marrakech. The only things missing are the fezzes. One by one they do their thing and leave. Sam finds an opening and makes his way up the step. The man who followed him in stands to his left. Sam feels a sharp prick to his lower back that makes him jolt. He almost loses control of his urine. He looks to his right first

– a man stands there urinating. He looks to the left and notices the man who'd arrived after him just stepping down from the trough. Tall and bulky, like a Sherman tank. Bald head, with a tattoo of a swastika dead-smack in the middle of his skull. Sam shakes his head, returning to the task at hand.

Kostas finally gets his chance to speak with Chip. He hugs the director and whispers congratulations into his ear. Smiles all around. The speaker comes to life. The awards are about to recommence. Everyone begins moving back into the foyer, hustling back to their seats.

Kostas looks around but doesn't see Sam anywhere. He's worried that he has fallen asleep somewhere. The amount of alcohol Sam has consumed could lead to many different scenarios. Let's hope falling asleep is the one that's happened. But Kostas doesn't have time to search now. Sam might have gone back to his seat for all he knows, so Kostas heads back in himself.

He sits down next to Nadia. She has reapplied her makeup. The thought of how beautiful she looks pops back into his head. He turns away so as not to make it too obvious. He can see from the corner of his eye that she is smiling at him. It's reassuring to know she isn't angry with him anymore.

After quite a few more formalities, awards, and hours later, the time has come for what everyone had been waiting for – the Academy Award for Best Actor. The building is packed with talented people, actors in general, but only one can win this category. There has never been a tie for first place in the Awards' history. Could tonight be different?

'And the nominees for Best Actor are… Paul Jacob, *Stirling Beauty*. McKenzie Lavender, *The Tomorrow People*. Brody Spencer, *Struggle Town*. Jasper Lonfiest, *War Within Us*. Arjun Kapoor, *The Railroad Tracks*. And Kostas Dellos, *The Hillside Murders*.'

The envelope is brought out to the presenter. A card is removed. The presenter looks up, directly into the camera and the words begin to leave his mouth.

'And the Oscar goes to—'

A gun goes off. The presenter collapses.

After a moment of shocked silence, the crowd starts to scream. The presenter lies on the stage, blood beginning to seep from under his head – what's left of it. Then a man walks onto the stage. He tells people to stay calm and to remain where they are. This is a hostage situation. Some try to run, but they're gunned down in cold blood. The crowd begins to yell once again.

Kostas is frozen, glued to his seat. Nadia grabs his hand in fear. They both know the man on stage.

It's Petros.

Chapter 21

This would make for a great movie, but in the movies people don't die for real. Makeup and fake wounds make them look dead. But this is real and people have died. Not coming back to make an appearance again. No makeup, no fake scars, no one screaming, 'Cut!' Here, there are real bullets, real wounds, and real people screaming.

Nadia reaches over and grips Kostas's hand. The tension makes Kostas's knuckles go white. She is fixated on the terror in front of her. Sweat beads in her hairline. He squeezes back, gently. To let her know he is there and feels what she is feeling. They don't dare speak, make noise or sudden movements. Fear has taken over their souls.

The crowd is hushed with another shot fired in the air. Everyone is told to keep quiet. Petros is in charge now. He is using a calm voice. He says 'please' before the words 'stay calm'. He also says, 'No one else will get hurt if you all cooperate.'

He has killed someone in cold blood, with hundreds of witnesses. Kostas suspects that there will be no witnesses remaining after all this. Terrorists cover their tracks. No one is getting out of there alive.

Petros begins to speak. 'There is no need to tell you who I am at this moment or who I am involved with. You will learn all that in time. I do know who most of you are though, which makes things more exciting. I have never been in a room with so many celebrities before. I feel honoured.'

All eyes are on him. He is the centre of attention, the main focal point in this room. He is the Messiah, and the guests his disciples. He has calmed the entire auditorium within minutes. Petros waves over to the right side of the stage. A gesture for someone to come towards him. Two male soldiers make their way onstage. He says something to them that no one else can hear. They bend over and grab an arm each of the presenter and drag his corpse off the stage. Blood smears along the way, leaving a bloody path.

Petros speaks again. 'Let's not end this excitement here, shall we? We've come here for awards, and awards we will give you. I'll call out some names. Whoever I call out, I want you to come onstage. Please don't hesitate. I don't like to be kept waiting.'

Everyone looks around. Something bad is going to happen. Names are called out.

'Paul Jacob, McKenzie Lavender. Please come up here.'

Heads begin to turn and two figures stand up from where they're seated, and make their way towards the stage. Both were close to the front so it doesn't take them long. They stand reasonably close to Petros, one on each side of him. He's smiling, a sadistic smile of a man who has control of the universe.

Without a word, he pulls a gun out, and points it at Paul Jacob's temple. Screams echo across the room. And just like that, without warning, brain matter is splattered across the stage. Skull fragments are sprayed into the first few rows. More screams continue. Petros turns to McKenzie and does the same. Both men brutally murdered in front of hundreds of staring eyes. The auditorium has erupted in screams once again. A nightmare happening right in front of them. Family and friends try to run onstage. They are gunned down. Panic has filled the room, and any movement will get you killed.

Nadia tries to stand but Kostas grabs her tightly. He tells her not to move with his eyes. *If you move, you die.* Nadia can sense the calmness in Kostas. One of them needs to step up.

It takes a while to settle the scared crowd. Bodies are dropping like flies. At this rate there won't be anyone left to hold hostage.

'They had no chance of winning. I did them a favour.' Petros looks into the crowd. 'Jasper Lonfiest and Kostas Dellos. Come on up.'

Nadia looks over to Kostas. This time Kostas doesn't look at her. He knows what's coming. Nadia does, too. Dying isn't the biggest problem – having Nadia witness it is. He always wanted to protect her from the evil that exists in the world, but today he's not even able to protect himself, and Nadia knows that. He looks over to his right and notices Jasper standing up. His partner is crying and holding his arm for dear life. Even God can't protect them now. Only a miracle can save them. Kostas hopes God isn't too busy. He needs him right now.

He's about to stand up when he notices someone stand about five rows ahead. A figure towering above the people seated. It's Sam Baker. He starts walking towards the stage.

Kostas is stunned. Why would he risk his own life for Kostas?

He looks over to Nadia. She mimes, 'Don't stand, don't stand.' He listens to her. Even if he wanted to, his legs prevent him from doing so.

Both men get to the stage at the same time. Jasper closes his eyes; Sam keeps his open. Jasper begins to cry; Sam smiles and starts whistling. Jasper drops. Sam turns and spits in Petros's face and yells, 'Fuck you, motherfucker!' before the shot rocks his head, and he too, crumples to the floor next to Jasper.

Tears form in Kostas's eyes. He squeezes Nadia's hand twice, trying to get her attention. She looks over.

'I have something to tell you. Something I need you to know about me,' he whispers.

'Tell me later. They might hear us.'

'Later might be too late. You need to know now.'

'What is it?'

But Kostas never gets the chance to tell Nadia what he wanted. Petros speaks, and he sounds angry. He knows that wasn't Kostas. He was double-crossed by the stunt double. Someone has tried to step in and impersonate Kostas. This has made Petros furious. He begins scouring the crowd with his beady, dangerous eyes, looking around for Kostas. He spots him. The look of anger turns to sorrow. He has just noticed who is clinging onto his arm. Now Nadia knows who Petros really is. He's a monster. No, he's worse than a monster; he is the Devil. Nadia feels the hatred build up inside her. She tenses up and, without noticing, she squeezes Kostas's hand hard. The pain makes him jerk.

A man with a personal bodyguard walks onto the stage. He doesn't look like much. Definitely not like a killer. He reminds Nadia of the uncle who all the nieces and nephews love; the uncle who would spend hours with them playing games. The bodyguard is another story. He looks like a killer.

He walks in front of Petros and steals the spotlight. The stage is all his. He taps the microphone twice before he opens his mouth to speak. 'I hope you are all comfortable. Please remain seated while I speak. No need to stand for me yet.'

Some stand in defiance.

'Don't make me repeat myself,' the man says. 'I don't give second chances.'

All sit but one. Brody Spencer.

'Sit down, you stupid fool,' whispers Kostas. He must have a death wish or something.

A bullet hits its mark. A bullseye, square between the eyes. The limp body of Brody crumples to the floor, coming to rest over a few chairs. Blood covers his face, making it unrecognisable. The exit wound has left a large hole in the back of his head, the bullet hitting a person three rows back, too. He joins Brody on the list of the dead.

'Now that I have your attention and you're all seated, I would like to introduce myself. My name is Jurgen Clive. Most of you would have heard of me, those who haven't, I suggest you ask the person next to you after I am done talking … if they are still alive. My friend JR here is one of the best, hence the reason why I have hired him. All this has been made possible because of him. We are part of a group called *Vierte Reich*, meaning The Fourth Reich. Like our predecessors before us, I believe we have the means to succeed in our big goals. Not to say the German Empire, Weimer Republic, and the Nazis fought for anything less. I just feel that our cause is substantially validated to succeed. Let me demonstrate our power. Miroslav, the sticky candy please.'

Miroslav digs into a bag that's draped over his right shoulder and removes a package. The parcel is wrapped like a gift. He holds it out in front of him, making no sudden movements. He doesn't want to drop it. Yet. Miroslav looks over to his boss, awaiting instructions.

'You are probably wanting to know what this is and what I'm going to do with it? Simple. I am going to blow this place up with all you in it if I don't get what I want. Simple, yes?'

Nothing in life is that simple. Kostas and everyone else knows that they're going to die there tonight. Unless someone does something about it.

As Jurgen continues talking, Kostas feels a nudge against his back. A voice speaks softly into his ear. An accent he can pick out of a line-up. It's Arjun Kapoor.

'Don't turn around. Just listen. I have a plan. Dangerous, but we have no time to plan anything else and I am not dying here today. I have a family to get to in Jaipur. There are tunnels under this building. They lead out to the water. If we can get to them then we are free. If not, then we are dead.'

'I prefer being free,' whispers Kostas.

'I prefer the same thing, my friend.'

'How are we going to find the entrance to the tunnels?'

'Lucky for you, I know a way in. An old friend has taken me for a tour down there once before.'

'We need to find the right time to do it—'

They're interrupted by a shot. They turn to see Jurgen holding his pistol in the air, smoke coming from the barrel. He's staring in their direction, but he doesn't have a clear view. Too many heads in the way.

'Now that I have explained about the bombs, I'm guessing your next question is why? Simple.'

Kostas is getting annoyed with this 'simple' bullshit. If only it were true, he would get the upper hand.

'The American government are always sticking their nose where it doesn't belong. They have done it so many times. The Middle-East is a prime example. Well, enough is enough. The Fourth Reich will not stand for that, and we are here to send them a message. A message that you will all be a part of.'

Jurgen looks behind him. He's looking for Petros. He must have ducked out back while Jurgen was explaining the bag of bombs.

'JR? Where are you. I want you to be here for the fun part.' A smile leaves his face while he looks around. Jurgen signals Miroslav over and whispers something into his ear. Miroslav puts the package back into his bag and walks off the stage. He stops, turns around, and walks back to Jurgen. He takes the bag off his shoulder and places it carefully onto the ground at the feet of his boss, though there's another bag on his other shoulder. Then Miroslav turns back and walks off the stage, losing himself amongst the crowd.

Kostas turns to Nadia. His eyes filled with worry, his palms and skin are sweaty. He knows there are only two ways out of here. One breathing and the other not.

'Nadia, there is something I need to tell you. I'm not sure how to say it, but I'll give it my best.'

Once again, Kostas is interrupted – this time by Arjun.

'Now is our chance. There are only two guards at the rear door. We distract them. Follow my lead.'

They take one last look around. Clear from both sides. Kostas grabs Nadia by the hand and leads her towards the door. He follows Arjun closely; other guests look on at what they're doing. A few catch on to the plan and follow the trio. They reach the back aisle – there are soldiers holding M16 rifles. They're spotted by the guards. The rifles come up, aimed at Arjun, who lifts his hands in defeat, surrendering to the enemy. They begin talking Thai, a language Arjun speaks fluently. He doesn't make it known but just smiles.

Arjun makes them believe they will head back to their seats. They walk up an aisle three rows from where they were seated. They stop in front of one of the chairs. The guards have turned away, making sure no one leaves from those doors. Arjun moves one of the chairs – the carpet is loose, and beneath it is a trapdoor. He lifts the latch; the door lifts up with ease.

One by one they climb down the ladder into darkness. Arjun goes in first, the light from his phone illuminating the path. His feet hit the concrete floor. Nadia goes in next while Kostas keeps watch. She is safely in the tunnel.

Kostas doesn't wait any longer. He makes his way in and closes the latch behind him. No one had noticed them go through the trapdoor because they had all turned to see others attempt the same thing that they tried, to leave from the rear door where the soldiers were standing guard.

He descends into complete darkness. 'Nadia, are you okay? Arjun? Nadia?'

The tunnel is silent. A vampire's paradise; pitch black. He can't even make out his fingers on the rungs. He finally gets to the bottom. He hears a noise, loud and close. A familiar sound; one he has come accustomed to.

He removes his phone from his pocket. Uses his thumb to bring the phone to life. He notices there's no reception down there. He also realises why Nadia and Arjun aren't responding.

There's a gun pointed at Nadia's head. The gun belongs to a killer. Miroslav.

Chapter 22

Kostas

I'm caught between a rock and a hard place. I feel the tightness in my chest, knowing the trouble we're in could be the last thing we ever encounter here today. Every move I make, every step I take, something always finds a way to block my path and stop me in my tracks.

The guy has a satchel over his arm and his gun pointed at Nads. He has a look on his face like he's not taking any prisoners.

I know he won't kill us, yet. He takes orders. He has made his way down here to find us, I'm quite sure of that.

'Moras da me pratis, sada.'

I look at him, confused. He has spoken in a language I don't understand. I know he understands English. His boss speaks to him in English. But this sounds Slavic. Nads looks at me for guidance which I'm unable to provide. It's literally foreign to me. I look at Arjun to see what he makes of it.

'I'm sorry, we don't understand,' he says.

'You come with me now.'

The beast speaks English. He has a strong accent that throws me off a little, but it's definitely Slavic. I have a friend from Serbia who sounds like that.

He waves the gun, pointing it to the left, indicating for us to start walking down the tunnel. The path is dark. Arjun leads the way, Nads next, me behind her, and then him. If anything happens, I'll be the first one to cop it. The goat being led to the slaughterhouse.

We've reached the end of the tunnel. A T-intersection. Left or right are the options. If only we could go up.

'Levo.'

I guess what he is saying. We turn left, but then Arjun stops abruptly.

'I have to tie my laces,' he says. I repeat it to the beast, explaining to him in mime. He stands about two metres away from me. We're too far to try anything stupid, too close to run away from him. I can get shot either way and I'm not planning on doing that today.

He responds by waving his gun. That must mean yes. Should I tell Nads now what I've wanted to tell her earlier? Secretly. I don't want anyone else to hear.

I hear a phone ring. I put my hand to my pocket. It's not mine. It's coming from behind me. It's the beast's phone. He slips it out of his jacket pocket, flips it open, and answers the call. The voice on the other end is calm. Almost soothing. The beast keeps repeating the same word. 'Da.'

I look at Arjun, direct him with my eyes to an entrance a few metres in front of us. He looks over towards it, looks back and shakes his head. Nads is trying to catch onto our secret conversation. Miming wasn't her strong point when playing charades. She would always forget that you weren't supposed to talk. We all had fun, lots of laughs at her expense. Now's not the time to speak.

'I need to pee.'

Nads's words leave me with my mouth open. I was hoping she would keep her mouth closed, not say a thing.

The beast looks confused.

'I need to pee, you know … um, toilet?' She makes a gesture with her thumb, sticking it out and placing it in front of her crotch, pretending it's a penis. She also throws in sound effects for good measure. 'Pssssssss.'

The beast finds that funny. I didn't know he had it in him. A smile and giggle. Nothing should surprise me anymore, but some things still do.

'Treba sacekati,' he says. 'Wait.'

He continues to speak Slavic, even though we don't understand him.

He waves the gun and we begin to walk again. We pass the door that I had pointed out to Arjun. It is padlocked shut. He must have known. The beast notices me looking at it. He lets out a grunt, then a laugh. He finds it funny. I don't. An urge to knock that smile off his face creeps in. First, I need to find a way to knock that gun out of his hand. That'll be a little trickier than the smile.

My eyes dart ahead. I notice Arjun picking up speed. *What's he up to?*

His feet move like Mumble, the penguin from *Happy Feet*. He's shuffling down the corridor, darkness making things a little harder to see where he's rushing to. His dark suit is not making things any easier. Before I know it, he's vanished. I look over my shoulder to see if the beast has noticed.

He has – the beast pushes past me, almost knocking me over and shoving Nads against the wall of the tunnel with his large frame. She bangs against it hard and slides down to her knees. The wind is knocked out of her. I stop and help her back up to her feet. Her breathing is staggered, gasping for air. Not much of it down here in the tunnels. I whisper softly to her.

'Are you okay?'

'I'm fine. Where is Arjun?'

'I'm not sure, but I hope he's found a way out. Help is what we need right now. We need to stay still and not move. He'll shoot us if we do.'

'Let's turn and go back the other way. We can outrun this guy.'

'We can't outrun bullets, Nads. It's too dangerous.'

'I'm scared, Kostas.'

I don't want to make her think that she is alone in that. 'I'm scared, too. We'll be okay if we play this out right.'

Now is the perfect time to tell her. I need to be quick about it before there's another interruption. 'Nads, I need to tell you something.'

'Oh, for fuck's sake, Kostas. Is now really the time? I'm about to piss my pants and I don't know if it's from fear or my bladder is just full. What is it?'

I try to find the right way to tell her that I'm a—

A loud bang echoes in the tunnel. The sound makes my ears ring. Deafness hollows my thoughts. Nads has her fingers over her ears. The smell of urine and the sound of hissing indicates that her bladder has just released. A puddle forms down by her feet.

A gun has been fired. My first initial thought is Arjun has been shot. The beast has a gun, Arjun doesn't. Silly fool. I told him not to run. He should have listened. Now he's dead. Fuck.

A light flicks on from the direction of the gunshot. I can see a figure walking towards us. A large figure. The beast.

But something is not right. He's staggering, not walking in a straight line. The light is reflecting from behind him. Then he's in clear view. His large body stands a few metres in front of us, staring directly into my eyes. Then, without warning, he collapses at our feet. Blood forms a pool beside his torso.

The beast is shot. The beast is dead. But how?

Another figure emerges from the dark holding a torch. They're walking towards us. A flashlight in his hand. It's Arjun! He's alive. A thousand questions rush into my head but I can only muster just one.

'How did you overpower him?'

'It wasn't me,' Arjun say. 'It was him.'

Out of the darkness steps another figure holding a gun. It's Petros.

Chapter 23

Why did you do it? Why did you help us?' asked Kostas.

A reasonable question considering the confrontation on Samui. A question any normal person would be asking considering the actions Petros has taken so far.

'I didn't like him that much. He was a thug.'

'Compared to you? From where I'm standing and what I have seen, you're no different.'

'I'm a hired gun, a hitman. There's a considerable difference between the two. I get paid to hurt people, a thug does it for pleasure.'

'Well, I don't think there is a difference.' says Arjun.

'If I were a thug, I would have helped him, not the other way around. I'm paid to kill people. You, my friend, better be careful what you say or you could still be one of them.'

Nadia breaks her silence. She couldn't hold her tongue any longer. 'You called out Kostas's name. You were going to kill him.'

'I was, but only because I have been paid to. I don't take pleasure in killing people. I'm not a sadist. I do it for the money. It's my job.'

'That's not a job. A job is where you wake up in the morning and get dressed in your best clothes, have coffee, toast, cereal or whatever tickles your fancy for breakfast, commute on public transport, the whole shebang of a routine. You are a killer, a thug, and someone I wish dead.'

Her words cut deep. Wounds that can never be healed. Petros knows the consequences with his line of work. No feelings for the victims. No remorse for the killing, no regrets once he's paid. But this is different.

He had feelings for Nadia. He still does. He did everything to protect her, and he still is. Nothing he says now will change how she feels.

'Regardless of what you think of me, I need to get you out safely.'

'Why should we even believe a word you tell us?' says Kostas.

'You don't. You just need to trust me, and you're in no position to doubt me.'

Time is running out. Eventually, someone will come looking for Miroslav. His body is taking up space on the cold concrete floor. Sounds begins to generate from behind them, unsettling the group. The four of them need to come up with an agreement to trust one another for enough time for them to get out of this hole, alive.

'What is your real name? Is it even Petros?' Nadia is not holding anything back. If there is one person who should be pissed, it's her. This man in front of her has lied multiple times. Does he even know how to be truthful?

'My name is Jim Reeves. Petros is a name I used in Greece. It's a long story that we don't have time for.'

'Okay, *Jim*. Once this is all over, you have some explaining to do. Then you can leave and do whatever you want. I just want to know why you lied to me.'

'I promise, I will explain my actions to you. But for now, we need to go.'

Petros – Jim – turns and takes off down the tunnel, the opposite direction from where they had come. The quickness of his actions doesn't give any of the others time to ask any more questions. He dodged one bullet, for now. He knows he has to answer more later, provided they get out of this alive.

He has a new mission. One that wasn't planned. He needs to get Nadia to safety. He never signed up for this. He doesn't give two fucks about the other two. He has made that quite clear. He won't think twice in killing Kostas and Arjun, or even himself, to save Nadia.

The trio follow their newfound alley, distancing themselves from the noise above them. Using their phone flashlights makes manoeuvring down the tunnel easier. The walls on either side stand tall. The path gets narrower the deeper they run. Air a little scarce, fear off the charts.

They move with super speed in stealth mode through the dark tunnel. There's a light ahead. They arrive at an adjoining tunnel that leads out to the right. Jim stops, and the others do, too. He looks down the tunnel to the right. Pitch black. He looks at the light in front of him.

'We head down this way,' he says while making a right turn down the dark tunnel. The others don't move from their spot.

'But the light is up ahead. Shouldn't we go for the light?' says Arjun. Nadia and Kostas nod.

'That's not the right way.'

'But the light?'

'It means nothing. There could be others there. People we're trying to avoid.'

'But you could be leading us to them for all we know.' says Kostas.

'Or I could be leading you to safety, for all you know.'

'I believe him,' says Nadia.

'After what he did up there?' says Arjun, pointing towards the ceiling. 'I'm trying to, but I'm having a hard time doing so.'

'Listen,' says Jim, 'by me helping you, and killing Jurgen's right-hand man, has put me in the same sinking boat you're in. Matter of fact, I'm in worse trouble than you would ever be in. My life in hiding is now my life on the run. You want to stay here, not follow me, be my fucking guest. But I'm not hanging around. If either of you want to stay with this dumb prick then that is on you, not me. I suggest you make that decision, I'm leaving in a minute, and I suggest you, Nadia, come with me.'

The situation has just moved up a notch. Fighting words from someone who has been in this position many times before.

Nadia looks at Jim. A connection crosses between them; a feeling they both felt many years ago in Greece. A feeling that could possibly get them out of this mess. Then she looks over to Arjun with soft, convincing eyes. 'We need to stick together. I feel it in my bones, Jim means what he is saying. He won't put us in any danger. I'm going with him.' 'I'm going with him, too, Arjun,' says Kostas. 'Come with us.'

Jim turns his back and starts walking. 'I'm leaving. Those who are coming with me, follow now.'

'Come, Arjun,' say Nadia and Kostas simultaneously.

They both turn and follow Jim; Arjun a fraction behind them. Into the darkness they go, not knowing where they'll end up.

A scream echoes from somewhere within the tunnel. Someone else is down there with them. A voice follows. Sounds German.

'Sie sind hier unten!'

'They know we're down here,' Jim says.

Chapter 24

Jurgen is waiting for news from Miroslav on the whereabouts of JR. The story on how Jurgen met Miroslav goes back many years, when Miro was a young boy back in Mokra Gora, Serbia. The meaning of Mokra Gora is 'wet mountain'. With a population of just over five hundred people, he was bound to find a young soldier to mould into a killing machine. Jurgen knew the village quite well. He spent three weeks there back in 1996, where he met the family who would produce this assassin known as *Ubica Boga* – God Killer.

Jurgen was there under orders. He had to lay low for some time for his crimes in Bosnia. The crimes were so horrific, the Hague had put out a warrant for his arrest, dead or alive. Jurgen would rather have that hanging over his head than a noose around his neck.

The decision to hide him in Serbia came from the officers above him. No one would look for him there, especially in Mokra Gora. The war between Serbia and Croatia had broken into a modern bloodbath. Bosnia had suffered a considerable number of casualties, which the Serbians had ordered. Jurgen Clive was a hero to them. Now he needed a God to look over him. The God he knew wanted nothing to do with him.

He stayed with Miroslav's family the entire time he was there. Miro's dad, Boris, struggled to provide for his family. A wife and four kids depended on him for their survival. Money hadn't come easy for the family, so Boris had no choice but to surrender to Jurgen's request. Jurgen had offered Boris \$100,000US to buy his eldest son, Miroslav. The catch behind the offer was if Boris had declined, Jurgen would kill his entire family and burn down the village, leaving no trace of his war crimes, but most importantly his DNA. Lose one child or lose an entire family, including himself. What would you do?

Jurgen took Miroslav in as his own and raised the boy in blood, sweat, and violence. By the time Miroslav was a teen, he knew nothing else but to kill, and kill for his family. Jurgen was now his family, and he wouldn't, and couldn't let anything happen to him. *Ubica Boga* was born, a new-age killer with nothing to lose.

Jurgen looks around to see if he could spot his God Killer. All he sees are scared lambs, and a few slaughtered ones. All exits are guarded, Wi-Fi has been cut so there is no communication with the outside world. Every guest needs to be accounted for. The only ones that are missing are Miro and JR.

It has been over an hour since the auditorium was placed under his control. A hush has come over the guests, jackets removed and ties undone. The air conditioning system has been switched off. The temperature rising to an unbearable state.

Tommy and his men are keeping the situation under control. Making sure there are no surprises from anyone trying to be Rambo. He has made it known to everyone that he is working with these terrorists.

One of the soldiers runs up and whispers something to Jurgen. He doesn't respond right away. He signals to Tommy to come over.

'They have located JR. He is down in some tunnels under this building. He is spotted with others. He's helping them escape. Did you know about these tunnels?'

'I heard of them but never been down. With my age and size, I no interest.'

'When were you going to tell me about them?'

'When you ask. Is my job keep you safe, this building secure. Not give you a history lesson on tunnels.'

The conversation is getting a little heated. Frustration on the face of Jurgen. Tommy smiling like a predator. Both men in a vulnerable state; they can kill the other in an instant.

Jurgen calls over four of his men and gives them instructions to head down there and kill anyone who isn't with them. He also tells them to keep an eye out for Miroslav. He's been missing for over twenty minutes. The men disperse and head in different directions with only one goal: find and kill the missing links. A mission they've carried out for their general many times before. Being in a foreign country is nothing new to them. Dealing with innocent people is also nothing new to them, but looking to possibly kill one of their own is. The orders have been given; the mission is underway. JR is now a targeted man.

'Commissioner, so there is no confusion, I need your men out of our way to commence stage two of this event. Please make sure all your men are at the exit points guarding anyone trying to leave or anyone trying to get in. Can you do that for me?'

'Yes, I can. This is why we here, is not?'

Tommy has a group of twenty hardened criminals made out as policemen on his payroll to sort through any orders he requires taken care of. In return, all of his hired soldiers and their families live comfortably and safe. A small price to pay for killing people you don't know.

Jurgen's men scatter throughout the inside of the building, looking for an entrance to the tunnels. They enter through doors that lead to nowhere. Doors that end in closets. Doors to toilets, doors to offices, doors to private function rooms.

Two of them enter through a door that leads them to a dressing room. Tuxedos and silk dresses hang from the hangers on portable garment racks. There's a rug in the middle of the room. The rug is slightly elevated. It seems a little odd to them. They inspect the rug.

There's a trapdoor under the rug. This could be the entrance to the tunnels. They discuss amongst themselves whether they should let the boss know what they have found. They decide to go down themselves without asking. Before they enter the underground compartment, they lock the door to the room. Making sure no one else enters after them. They both disappear, closing the trap-door behind them.

Tommy makes his way to the front of the building. The doors are heavily guarded by his men. He can see the boat that brought them all to the island. People walking around on the docks, oblivious to what is happening in the building. From that distance they look like ants. He also notices reporters hanging around outside the main doors. He tells his men to open the door to let him out.

He calls the reporters over and tells them that everything is going well. He also tells them that there is no need for them to stay at the front of the building as it will go on for a while longer and no one will be coming out soon. It would be a waste of time just being there. He instructs the media to head back to the boat and he will radio in advance when the guests will commence to exit the building. The logic behind all this is that the less people hanging around, the less of a threat this operation will be.

Louise Tamaraporn is suspicious with this request. Something doesn't feel right. She makes her way towards the boat with the others, but before they reach the pier, she bends down to tie the straps on her shoes and tells the others she will catch up to them. Once the others are out of sight, she removes her shoes and makes her way back to the building through the garden, holding her shoes in one hand while using her other hand to clear branches from the path. She's unsure what she is getting herself into, but if she's going to get the truth, then this is what she needs to do. A wildcat amongst the jungles of Africa, with lions and tigers as her enemy.

Jim hears commotion and speeds things up. There is an elbow in the tunnel just up ahead. The others are close behind. He spots flashlights that are shone down the tunnel towards them. They make the elbow just in time not to be spotted. Safe for the time being.

Jurgen's soldiers are in the tunnels. They come to a halt when they spot a body lying motionless on the floor.

'Sie sind hier unten! Sie sind hier unten!'

They check the pulse of their fallen comrade, Miroslav. No pulse. He's dead.

'Wir mussen es dem Chef sagen. Er muss er wissen.'

They take off back up the same path they had come. Up the steep ladder and through the trapdoor. They place the rug back over it and unlock the door. They make it back onto the stage. Jurgen is standing there with his eyes closed, listening to some classical music that is being played over the large speakers. There is a silent debate on who will tell Jurgen that Miroslav is dead; both men stand next to him, not saying a word. Waiting to be spoken to first. Sweat begins to form under their eyes. The younger of the two takes a step back, distancing himself from his friend.

The other soldier leans in and whispers the news into Jurgen's ear, making sure no one else can hear what has happened. Jurgen's eyes open, wide and focused, and tears form. He has just learnt that his *Ubica Boga*, his God killer, his adopted son, is dead.

Jurgen doesn't move. He stands there staring into the eyes of his soldier, clenching his jaw. Any tighter and it would break. Looking deep into his soul, knowing whatever happens from this moment on, it will be done without Miroslav.

Jurgen lets out a scream that could wake up the dead. He pulls out his pistol and shoots his soldier in the head. The blood splatters all over Jurgen's face.

'Find them and kill them all, NOW!'

Chapter 25

There is a faded light coming from a crack in a door. Jim is not sure where this leads but it's a risk he is willing to take. Anything to get them out of the dark tunnels.

They reach the door and stand there. Their own heavy breathing is the only thing they can hear. Jim peeks through the door. The light is coming from a tall free-standing lamp. He can also see a desk in there. No one in the seat. He pushes the door open, far enough to get a better look inside. The room is empty.

They all walk in and close the door behind them. Before closing the door, Kostas looks down the tunnel to see if anyone is coming. It's dark and quiet.

Once inside the room, they look around for anything to defend themselves with against the terrorists. It's an office, not an armoury. The only potential weapon is an umbrella. Useful in a storm, not against bullets. On the desk there are papers neatly stacked, a laptop that is open but not powered up, and a pen holder full of pens and pencils. They do say a pen is mightier than a sword but not in this case. Kostas takes one anyway and places it in his pocket.

Nadia makes her way to a wardrobe. The doors are locked but the key sits in the lock. She turns it and the door flings open with force. She steps back and screams before placing her hand over her mouth.

A body tumbles out of the wardrobe. He's a Thai man, his throat slit from one ear to the other. No blood, though. He must've been killed elsewhere and brought here to dispose of. Kostas puts his arms around Nadia and turns her away from the body. He hugs her, and she squeezes him tightly, her face buried into his chest. Jim's eyes burn a hole through the back of her head. Kostas watches him watch her.

'We need to move out of here. I don't want to end up like him,' says Arjun, pointing at the dead man.

Jim looks for a way out. There is a door to the right of the wardrobe. He walks over to it and turns the handle. It's unlocked. He opens the door and notices stairs leading up.

'I'm going up to see where these stairs lead to. It would be safer down here for the time being. Lock both doors and don't open to anyone.'

He closes the door; they can hear his footsteps going up the stairs. The noise vanishes within seconds. They're all alone now, in a room with no protection, waiting for Jim to return. Can they trust him? Probably not, but what choice do they have? They wait with anticipation.

Jurgen has relaxed slightly after gunning down one of his men. Blaming him for the death of his adopted son. Jurgen's eyes are filled with flames, like a dragon looking to burn down the castle that's holding his princess. He knows things have shifted away from what their plans were; he's now in uncharted waters without his right- and left-hand men, Miroslav and JR. Someone close to him has changed the dynamics of this attack, putting a spanner in the works.

His closest friend and fellow sociopath has turned against him. He needs to find JR and skip the part about asking questions. He trusted this man with his own life. It must have been JR who was responsible for killing Miroslav, which means he won't feel any remorse when he kills JR. He will pull the trigger himself. He wants to be the last thing JR sees as his eyes close for the last time.

Jurgen sends out a request to have Tommy come back. Plan B needs to begin. Jurgen feared that something like this might happen, but he never in his wildest dreams would have pictured JR to be the traitor.

Tommy makes his way through the heavy double doors. He has his right-hand man next to him. The behemoth body of the commissioner trots along the path like an elephant led to centre stage of a circus. Jurgen is the ringmaster about to give his animal a command.

'We are moving to Plan B. We need to get started before things change again. JR has betrayed us. Even if that turns out false, we need to dispose of him and finish the job.'

'Where is he?'

'Missing. These fucking tunnels are going to ruin everything,' says Jurgen, not hiding any of his anger.

Tommy's smile has faded. 'I have sent some of my men down tunnels to smoke out fox. I commence next stage. Where is bag with bombs?'

Jurgen looks around him, his eyes scouring the floor for the bag. Miroslav had one of the bags with him around his shoulder. The other bag is sitting there beside a body. Miro must still have the other one with him, down in the tunnels. Someone else has access to the bombs.

'Fuck. Fuck! Tell your men down in the tunnels that Miroslav has the other bag with him. They need to find him and the bombs.'

'Why you not call him on radio?'

'Because he won't hear me. He is dead.'

A concerned look twists the commissioner's face. The plan is beginning to crack. Jurgen needs to correct it before it all goes wrong. Regardless of the plan they go with, everyone must die.

The commissioner approaches one of the guests who had won an award earlier in the night. He's sitting with his wife. His hands are clamped around the award, protecting it like a mother would her child.

Tommy instructs his men to grab Chip Longmuir and drag him along with them. The award drops out of his hands. The metal makes a loud noise when it hits the floor.

Chip's wife begins to cry. She has a fair idea what they might do to him. These people have proven to be brutal. She begs for his release, crying and holding onto Tommy's leg. Tommy dismisses her and laughs in her face.

'Pathetic American,' he says.

Someone helps her up off the floor. Chip vanishes through the main doors and falls victim to this group. She sits and stares into space; voices not registering at all. Her man has been whisked away, most likely to be killed.

An explosion rocks the entire building. The wall is pushed inwards, the doors are flung off the hinges, the two soldiers guarding the doors fly through the air and land in the fourth row. Screams fill the auditorium. Bodies are tossed around.

The wall comes crashing down behind the back rows on people. They're buried under the heavy, thick wall. Smoke and dust floats through the air. A fire has started in the foyer. The windows have shattered into tiny pieces, glass flying through the air like sharp missiles. Bodies lie on the ground, inside the building and out. Devastation has rocked the island. Authorities won't be too far away now. Jurgen needs to make his way out of there.

He knows his plans are ruined. Plan C kicks in: Get the Fuck Out of Here.

As he turns, he runs into someone's thick chest. Jurgen looks up, his eyes wide with shock. Standing right there in front of him is Jim. Hanging over his shoulder is the other bag of bombs. Anger begins to flare up in Jurgen, but he doesn't have the upper hand anymore.

'Hello, Jurgen. The show is over.'

Louise finds a door to the side of the building that is being occupied by two soldiers. They're smoking. She hides behind one of the bushes and waits for an opportunity.

The men finish their cigarette and turn to head back in. They open the door wide and step inside. Louise quickly rushes out of the bush and meets the door before it closes. She had picked up a branch and has jammed it into the gap. She waits a few seconds in case the soldiers had noticed the door not closing before heading in.

It looks like a rear entrance to the stage. She keeps her phone in her pocket. It's already set on silent. The soldiers are up ahead. Music drifts down a staircase to the left.

Then the building rocks. Something has hit it with a huge force. The walls all rattle and the roof sounds like it's going to collapse. She needs to get out of there right away, but she is stopped at her tracks when a hand wraps around her mouth. She is dragged into a room and the door closes.

Jim has a gun pressed up against the temple of Jurgen. The metal tip is flush on his skin. One move and his brain will be sprayed across the front row. Jurgen knows better than to upset a man who has nothing to lose. He is in no position to make any commands, but he can't help a bit of sarcasm.

'Welcome back, JR. I was so worried you were going to miss all the fun.'

'I wouldn't miss it for the world.'

'I can see that, only, you were meant to be by my side. What made you change your mind?'

Jim thinks to himself how much he should tell Jurgen. He has men all over this joint. *If I tell him about Nadia, he might have her hunted down like a rabbit and killed.* He needs to choose his next words carefully.

'I guess you can say I saw the light.'

'We both know that is not true. You are as religious as the Devil himself, JR. Try again.'

'Even the Devil believes in something, Jurgen.'

'Yes, that is true. But the thing they believe in is evil. You are evil, yet you hold a gun to my head. I am not an angel. I am as evil as you are.'

'You're more evil, and totally fucked in the head. You don't have an innocent bone in your body and you will burn in Hell for that.'

Both men fall silent. Staring into the eyes of evil. Who will blink first? The audience watch with anticipation, like a scene from a movie unfolding right before them.

'We have come here with a plan,' Jurgen says. 'You are going against this plan and the people above us will not be happy. We are both in danger now. You know this, yes?'

'All I know is that *your* life is in danger right now. The present is all I'm thinking about. We need to stop what we're doing. We can both get out of this, alive. Think about what we can do together, as a team, making things right again. For the good – we can take down the top level.'

'You are talking like a desperate man. One who values his life. Those thoughts will get you killed. I am who I am – a killer. I cannot change that and neither can you. Just in case you have forgotten, you are a killer, too. The worst kind.'

'We can change. I will change and I will pay for my sins separately, at another time and place.'

Jurgen takes a breath. 'I need to ask you something.'

'What?'

'Before I kill you, I need to know what made you change your mind? Surely the Devil didn't finally make a deal with God, did he?'

'Let's just say I was visited by an angel. An angel I should have listened to many years ago.'

The stage is rocked, the walls begin to collapse and the crowd scream frantically. The boards holding up the stage have become loose. An explosion has rocked the venue. Jim loses his balance and falls. A beam swings from the ceiling and comes crashing down, hitting Jim in the shoulder. His gun is knocked out of his hands. The bag with the bombs falls to the ground. He looks around and sees Jurgen kneel down and remove a pistol from around his ankle. His reliable Glock 43 is now in his hand and pointing towards Jim.

Jim knows there is no way out of this. His former friend, now foe, is not someone who gives chances. Jim senses his nine lives are about to be used up all at once. Only a miracle will save him from this.

'Isn't it funny how things can turn from good to bad in a flash … or a blast of a bomb.'

'You win, Jurgen. You always do.' Jim sounds defeated.

'Yes, I do. But this one is not for me. This one is for Miroslav. You will meet him sooner than you expected my friend. And I'll see you in another life.'

In a last-ditch effort, Jim opens his hand and shows a device in his palm. It's a trigger the size of a lighter with a yellow button on top. He presses it. The bag containing the bombs begins to beep.

'You fool! What have you done? You will kill us all!'

'See you in the next life, Jurgen.'

Louise looks over her shoulder. It's Kostas. He removes his hand from her mouth. Arjun Kapoor is there, too, and a woman she doesn't recognise. She's relieved it's them and not the soldiers.

Kostas introduces Louise to Nadia. They give each other a nod.

'Now, where to from here?' says Nadia.

'I saw two soldiers walk up some stairs behind the stage,' says Louise. 'I also know where there is an exit to outside. We should get out of this building and back to the boat.'

'There are a lot of people in the auditorium who need saving,' Kostas reminds them. 'I think you guys should leave, save yourselves. I will head deep into the building to see what I can do.'

'Are you crazy?' says Nadia. 'Do you have a death wish? We all need to get out of here. I'm not leaving without you.'

'Kostas, don't be a hero. Come with us and save yourself,' Arjun states, concerned.

'I can't. I have an obligation I need to carry out. An itch that needs scratching, if you know what I mean.'

They all look at each other. Nadia sees a look on her ex-husband's face she hasn't seen before. A look that tells her to trust what he's doing.

'We'll wait for you outside,' she says. 'Please be safe.'

She leads the others to the door and opens it, but she is pushed back and knocked over, hitting the wall with great force. She falls to the ground, dazed.

A couple of soldiers have burst through the door. One soldier reaches out and puts his hands around Arjun's throat. Caught off-guard, Arjun does the only thing he can and grabs the soldier around the waist. He leans back and forces them both to fall over a chair. The soldier loses his grip.

The other soldier heads over to Louise. He hasn't noticed Kostas in the corner. He's in the shadows, like a ghost. He makes his move. He leaps over the fallen chair and rams his shoulder into the soldier's side, crushing his ribs in the process. The crunch is so fierce, the soldier's head collides with the corner of the desk as he falls to the floor. Blood starts pouring out of a large gash that has opened up like a cracked watermelon. The soldier is down and it doesn't look like he'll be getting up anytime soon.

Arjun gets his bearings back and moves away from the other soldier. Before the soldier gets back up to his feet, Nadia comes in and smashes the chair over his head like a scene from *WWE*. Both soldiers are out cold. In normal circumstances, this would be a criminal offense. In Thailand, this offense will get you jail time or possibly death. At this point, it's the survival of the fittest. Do whatever it takes to stay alive.

The corridor is clear. Louise leads Nadia and Arjun towards the exit, and Kostas heads in the opposite direction towards the stairs that lead up to the top level. Nadia glances back towards Kostas. He vanishes from her sight. He had wanted to tell her something important. If something happens to him, she will never know what it was. She turns back and continues after the other two.

They reach the exit door in no time. They look around, making sure no one has followed them. It all looks clear. They can almost smell freedom. A metal door stands between them and the outside world. A way out of this nightmare. Fresh air, cool breeze – more likely humidity. Anything besides the smell of death will do.

Louise tries to push the door open but it's locked. She tries again. The door is not budging. Arjun pushes to the front and tries with his shoulder. He uses all the strength and energy he can muster. The door is sealed shut.

'It must be jammed from the explosion,' says Nadia.

'There has to be another way out,' responds Arjun.

'Move. Keep trying. Keep fucking trying,' says Louise as she uses both hands to try and wedge the door open. She gives up with her hands and begins using her feet to kick the door. The loud bangs echo in the hallway. If she keeps going, someone is sure to hear it and come down, spoiling their escape.

A door opens to their right. A woman's voice hisses at them. 'Stop making all that noise, lady. Are you trying to attract attention?'

It's Lesley Kara. She's holding a stick in her hands. Actually, a leg of a table that she has broken in half. 'Quick, come in here with us,' she says, 'it's safer than being out there.' She ushers them through and locks the door behind her.

A party of eight makes up Lesley's posse. Five women and three men. The only person they recognise is Lesley.

'How did you get down here?' Lesley asks.

Nadia responds. 'One of the terrorists helped us.' She looks over to Arjun, trying to signal to him not to mention who it was.

'What was that loud bang we heard earlier?' says one of the other women, dried blood on her forehead and a bruise beginning to show under her eye.

'We believe it was a bomb that went off,' says Arjun. 'The entire building is in danger of collapsing. We need to find a way out.'

'The only way out is back from where we came from,' says one of the men, short and stumpy, face full of fear.

'That's not an option,' says Nadia. 'You saw what went on up there. If we get caught, we won't survive. The only way out is through that exit door out there.'

'Then we need to head out there now and get that damn door open.'

They all agree and head towards the door. As they open the door to their room, another noise rocks the building, this one louder. The walls shake, and the ceiling begins to fall away.

'The building is collapsing,' Arjun yells. 'Quick, run!'

The exit door is no longer jammed because of this second explosion. Out in the hallway, it all goes quiet for a second. Then the building begins collapsing.

Three minutes earlier

Kostas makes his way to the top of the stairs. The door is unguarded and unlocked. He opens it slightly to peek through. He's on the stage behind the back curtain. No one else is around. He moves forward and closes the door slightly, leaving it a few inches ajar, just in case he needs to make a run for it.

There's screaming and loud rumbling noises coming from the other side of the curtain. He walks up to it and kneels down to look under it. Jim is lying on the ground, clutching a bag. Jurgen is standing above him with a gun in his hand, pointed directly at Jim.

Kostas needs to think fast. He doesn't have any time to waste. He scours the room and notices the far wall has collapsed. Bodies are scattered on the floor. Those still alive are hiding under their chairs. He needs to move now.

Kostas gets to his feet and feels his way across the curtain, trying to get through undetected. Before he can, a pair of large hands grasp his head. He gets tossed back from the curtain. He hits the floor with a thud, his head smacking the ground. Wetness trickles from above his right eye. He can smell the familiar metallic odour. Blood.

He looks up to see who threw him across the room like a ragdoll. It's Police Commissioner Tommy Jandocsuk. The most corrupt individual in the whole of Thailand. He's here in the flesh and is about to unleash his 300-pound body onto Kostas.

Tommy moves forward and reaches down to pick up Kostas, which he does with ease. His paw-like hands are now around the throat of Kostas, trying to cut off the circulation to his brain. If Kostas doesn't get out of his grip, he'll pass out within seconds. The fingers are squeezing tighter, air beginning to flow slower, his vision becomes blurry. Kostas is fading, and fading fast. How does one think in a situation like this?

Survival of the fittest. He closes his eyes and puts his hand into his jacket pocket, and retrieves the pen he'd grabbed from the office downstairs. He places it between his fingers, opens his eyes, and looks directly into the commissioner's. Without hesitation, he raises his right hand as far as he can and, with brute force, drives the pen straight into Tommy's eye. It goes more than halfway into his sweaty head. Tommy's other eye widens with shock and pain. He screams and lets go of Kostas. His limp body crashes to the floor.

The commissioner is squealing in pain. Blood gushes from his eye. His body is shaking, convulsing, ready to drop. The pen has most likely penetrated his brain. He hits the floor with a thunderous bang and goes still. The commissioner has corrupted his last event.

What do you know? The pen *is* mightier than the sword.

Kostas gets to his feet, trying to catch his breath and bring it back to a normal rhythm. He still has a job to do. He runs through the curtains towards Jurgen just as the gun goes off. Jurgen has shot Jim in the abdomen. Jim yells in pain.

Kostas notices something in Jim's hand. It's a lighter, he thinks, but when he looks more closely and sees that it's not a lighter but some sort of device. He's going to blow up the building!

Kostas continues running towards them. Jurgen turns and sees Kostas running his way. He lifts the gun. A shot is fired.

But the shot is not from Jurgen's gun. Kostas stops and looks over to his right. There is a man pointing a gun towards Jurgen. The bullet has hit him in the shoulder, making the gun fling out of Jurgen's hands. He collapses to the ground not far from Jim.

The man with the gun is Chaiyo, Jim's loyal soldier. They give each other a nod and Chaiyo turns and leaves. His job here is done.

Kostas looks over to Jim. He mouths something to Kostas. 'Go, now.'

Kostas looks at the bag, then turns and runs towards the curtain. He makes it through before a large explosion throws him forward.

Everything goes dark. The building comes down.

Epilogue

Kostas

Five days later

No one knew exactly what had happened that evening on Phi Phi Island. Five days on, and they're just getting to the bottom of the rubble. Bodies are being recovered and identified by loved ones. Others mutilated beyond recognition, awaiting DNA results to find out who they are. Body parts, clothing, accessories all hold key evidence.

The survivors will go through months, possibly years of therapy. Some might be able to talk about the horror that unfolded, others will probably fold up and die, taking their thoughts with them. We all have secrets, but if you were involved, would you talk? I guess time will tell. That's all they have now.

Doctors have spoken to me and cleared me of any serious injuries. I can't speak on behalf of some of the others. Some of their injuries are so horrific, it's unfathomable.

Lesley Kara made it out alive. She was thrown out of the doorway by a falling wall and pinned between the wall and a mahogany wardrobe. The hardwood saved her. Now I know why tables that are made from this material are so expensive. She crawled to safety after the blast. Someone from above was looking out for her.

She saved many others who were in that room with her that night. She led a group of frightened guests and made sure she did everything in her power to keep them safe. Unfortunately, some weren't lucky. Five from that group perished when the walls and roof collapsed. It saddened me to hear that.

Lesley was airlifted to Phuket Hospital and from what I've been told she's doing well. A broken leg and dislocated shoulder for her heroic effort.

Nadia made it out. She was dug free a few days ago. They discovered her under a heap of rubble near the exit of the building. Both her legs had been crushed, and she was found unconscious. She was flown to Bangkok General Hospital where she was taken into surgery to relieve the swelling around her brain. She remains in an induced coma. Her fighting spirit and will to live for her daughter is no doubt what's keeping her alive. Jemima, Ron, and Laura have all flown in from Melbourne to be by her side.

Her phone was in her pocket when she was rescued. It hadn't been damaged at all. Her body had protected it from the falling rubble. There was one unread message from an unknown number.

> I'm sorry for what I have caused. I'm sorry you were involved. If you read this then that means you are safe and made it out alive.
>
> There's nothing I can do to make this right. I hope what I'm about to do will at least make it right in your eyes. That's

all that matters to me. I had an angel look out for me, now that angel is looking over you.

Goodbye for now. I will see you again, somewhere.

Petros

Authorities couldn't trace the phone number. It was from a burner phone. The name isn't coming up on any databases. It's a mystery and will remain that way until Nadia pulls through; if she pulls through.

Arjun wasn't so lucky. He died on that dreadful night trying to save the others. A wall had come loose and was about to block the exit. Arjun had quickly overturned a table and used his body to lodge it upright against the wall. He held it there until most of them got out. It ended up being too much for him, and he perished for his troubles. He died not knowing whether he won the award for Best Actor. Something that might be written on his gravestone one day. May he rest in peace.

The body of Tommy Jandocsuk was removed from the rubble yesterday. Some of his men surrendered to authorities and told their side of the story. They wanted to do the right thing by talking. They explained the entire plan step by step, who was involved, and why they had done it. It took twelve months to plan, and it still ended badly.

Tommy was stripped of all titles. An inquest into his corrupt life will begin next week. A twenty-year affair with corruption, extortion, prostitution, trafficking, and murder, to name just a few of his crimes, which will be the highlight of the media once this unfolds.

A pen was lodged into his eye. That was what caused his death, not the collapse of the building. Nothing further will be investigated about that.

Jeff's body was found by fishermen off the coast of Samui. The fishermen had hauled the lifeless body on deck and noticed he was fully-clothed. His throat had been slit.

There were over five hundred people at the event that night. Guests, hosts, workers, and media. Some were invited, others invited themselves. The majority had a right to be there, others no right at all. And, at the end of it all, what did they really achieve? Nothing but a sad story that will be talked about for many years to come. This group might have perished trying to prove their point but there are many more building as we speak, trying to reignite a cause that no one else believes in.

Jim Reeves and Jurgen Clive were never recovered. There is no physical evidence they were even there. Verbally, witnesses have seen and acknowledged what they did, but their bodies weren't found. A mystery? Maybe. The hunt for them still goes on.

Yesterday, the rescue team and volunteers who were sifting through the rubble had located the envelope that contained the winner for Best Actor. The Academy said they will announce it live on TV. I wonder who won.

As for me …

There was something I needed to get off my chest. Something I needed to tell Nads. I never got that chance. I won't have to mention anything now. The cat isn't out of the bag yet.

The door opens and a nurse walks in. He's smiling excitedly.

'Detective, did you hear? Did you hear who won? It was just announced. I am so happy. *You* won, detective! Best Actor. You won!'

Acknowledgments

This is the part I don't need to think too hard about. There are a handful of people I want to mention who have contributed to this book.

First and foremost, my publisher and friend, Kev Howlett. You and the team at Busybird Publishing have made this all come to life. The watchful eye from above lends a special hand in all this – thank you, Blaise.

My wonderful and creative editor, Laura, for your bright and inspiring ideas to make this sound even better than it was. Working with you has made this process so much easier.

My old school mate and fellow author, Les Zig, for your insight and lessons on writing. Having you read my stories and give me your honest feedback made me see it from another angle.

My beautiful fiancé and soulmate Annwen for proofreading this book. The changes have made a huge difference to my story. It's made it sound even more dramatic. You are my rock.

To Karen Kirby, my Kazma-in-law, I want to say thank you for creating the cover for this book. It's exactly what I was looking for.

Love your work and the love you show me. It goes both ways.

My mother-in-law, Kay Groves, for your second edit and opinion on this book. As a retired teacher, what you told me about using the proper tense and grammar brought something to the table I hadn't known. Your support is much appreciated.

A big thank you goes out to the talented '*Hand Print*' artist Alby Finn Nash. The shape, size and perfect angles brings this cover to life. You're a Star.

To my family and friends, I want to say a big thank you for your current and ongoing support. It takes time to write a book; it takes a lifetime of love to accomplish it.

Now for my next project. It's called *The Crossword Killer.* It's a sequel to *The Full Moon Murders.* Just when you thought it was over … think again.

Standby for something out of this world.

About the Author

C on Shalevski was born in Melbourne to a Greek mother and Macedonian father.

Drama, reading, and writing were school hobbies that he never grew out of. His favourite genre is crime/thriller.

He is also an accomplished professional wrestler and storyteller. He lives with his beautiful family and his pooch Arlo in Melbourne.

The Invitation is his second book following his debut novel *The Full Moon Murders*, which was released in 2022.

The
Full Moon
Murders

Con Shalevski

Under the full moon
on the busy streets of Melbourne,
a killer prowls …

Every month under the light of the full moon, a predator strikes. Victims are being stalked across Melbourne, their final moments filled with terror and claws. And it's up to Detectives Willem Natloz and Spiro Petridis to track the monster down before it strikes again.

Chasing bloody pawprints and shadowy figures from the bustling CBD to rural New South Wales, the detectives are forced to confront their own fears and past traumas to uncover the secrets surrounding this sinister case. And when one of the detectives goes missing, it will take fresh blood on the investigating team to bring this killer to justice.

A spooky debut from Con Shalevski, The Full Moon Murders is a must-read for lovers of detective tales with a supernatural twist.

'This is a book you won't be able to put down, an amazing story with great characters and a twist you won't see coming at the end.'
– Natalie
Independent Reviewer